SHADOW FAMILY

SHADOW FAMILY

Miyuki Miyabe

Translated by Juliet Winters Carpenter

KODANSHA INTERNATIONAL
Tokyo • New York • London

Originally published by Shueisha, Tokyo, in 2001 under
the title *R.P.G.*

Distributed in the United States by Kodansha America,
Inc., and in the United Kingdom and continental Europe
by Kodansha Europe Ltd.

Published by Kodansha International Ltd., 17–14 Otowa
1-chome, Bunkyo-ku, Tokyo 112–8652, and Kodansha
America, Inc.

First edition, 2004
ISBN 4–7700–3002–9
10 09 08 07 06 05 04   10 9 8 7 6 5 4 3 2 1

www.kodansha-intl.com

Role-playing: a method of learning in which real-life situations are acted out; by playing various imaginary roles, participants master techniques of problem-solving.

Poster: Kazumi   10/08   20:15
Title: I'm in shock

I got my midterms back. What a disaster! I studied really hard, so when I saw my grades I couldn't believe it. Now I have to go in for a talk with the teacher. This is so unfair. It's not like I goof off or anything. Lots of other kids do, so why am I the one whose grades suck? Dad told me if I tried my best it would pay off in the end, but isn't that just a big lie? I'm so upset I can't sleep.

Poster: Dad   10/08   23:38
Title: Cheer up

Kazumi, I know how hard you studied for those tests. It's a shame you didn't get better grades. But I meant what I said—hard work does pay off in the end. Those classmates of yours who you think are goofing off might be hitting the books on the sly. Did you ever think of that? Anyhow, if you ask me it's a mistake to worry about how you stack up against others. Just focus on how you yourself are doing.

Is that talk going to be with your homeroom teacher? It's time you went over your college plans with him, anyway. If a third person can be present, I'd like to attend. Be sure to fill me in. And try not to feel too bad.

1

A light rap sounded, and the meeting room door swung open. Etsuro Takegami stood up, his metal chair scraping against the floor. Before he could open his mouth, Chikako Ishizu said, "It's been a long time." She was standing by the door, head lowered politely. When she raised her head again, though, she was beaming. Not a trace of awkward formality.

"Over fifteen years." Takegami responded with a warm smile of his own as he made his way around the long desk and crossed the room to greet her.

Detective Tokunaga, drawn to his feet by Takegami's example, looked on with interest. The young policewoman who'd accompanied Chikako into the room backed off a step, and stood crisply erect. Definitely nervous.

"Last night I got out an old diary and checked," Takegami went on. "It's exactly fifteen years and eight months since we worked together."

Chikako's full cheeks relaxed, and she stuck out her right hand. Takegami shook it warmly.

"That long?" she said. "It's good to see you still on the job. How's the family?"

"Fine. My wife sends her greetings."

Chikako looked pleased. "Tell her that potato omelet she gave me the recipe for is still a huge hit with my family."

A smile flickered over the serious-looking policewoman's face. Chikako introduced her. "This is Patrol Officer Mikie Fuchigami of Suginami Precinct."

Officer Fuchigami saluted with a click of heels. "How do you do? Pleased to meet you, sir."

She was tall. A good five foot eight, with an athletic build.

Chikako added, "After the murder, she helped with the stepped-up patrol around the Tokoroda house. She stayed there nights with me, and got to know Kazumi. For a while you were escorting her to and from school, weren't you?" She looked to the younger woman for confirmation.

The answer came briskly. "Yes, that's right. But only for a few days."

Takegami nodded. "Glad you came along, Officer. It'll be good for Kazumi to see a familiar face today."

"Yes, sir. Thank you, sir."

Her tone was businesslike, and yet at this unexpected show of cordiality Officer Fuchigami turned becomingly pink. Takegami had a daughter about her same age, to whom shyness was unknown. He found the young policewoman's ingenuousness refreshing.

"Where's Shimojima?" he asked.

They settled into chairs around the meeting table, Tokunaga included. Chikako answered the question. "In the chief's office, on the phone with Superintendent Kasai." She gave a shrug.

"Going over the plan?"

"Mm-hm. The super's been for it all along, so no worries there. The one with cold feet is the chief."

"You can't really blame him," Tokunaga said with a dry chuckle. "A stunt like this *is* pretty off the wall."

"Listen to you!" Chikako retorted good-humoredly. "A fine way to talk. You were all gung-ho before."

The two had known each other only a few days, but they seemed completely at ease together. Fifteen years and eight months was long enough for a bewildering array of changes to occur in anyone's life, Takegami mused, but Chikako seemed the same as ever. He recalled that back on the arson squad of the Tokyo Metropolitan Police Department, her nickname had been "Ma."

"Well, it does sound like it's going to be rather fun," Tokunaga said, still chuckling, and then caught himself. "Sorry, that was inappropriate. I apologize."

Chikako gave him a smile. "By the way, what about the stake-out? Have you—"

Takegami quickly cut in. "We've contacted our man. He's all set."

"Someone from your team, I hear."

"Name's Torii. A solid guy. You can count on him."

The phone rang. Officer Fuchigami sprang to her feet, picked up the receiver, said a few words, and then quickly looked over at Takegami. "It's Captain Shimojima, sir," she said. "He wants to see you in the Police Chief's office."

"Right." Takegami slapped his hands on his knees, and heaved himself up. "It's almost showtime. Might as well pay the producer a call."

This comment too was inappropriate, but Takegami made it on purpose. Everyone understood perfectly. They were all acting casual, but under the surface everyone was on edge, poised for action, as he well knew.

2

It had happened twenty-two days before, on the evening of April twenty-seventh.

Several people were quarreling loudly in a residential quarter in 3-chome Niikura, Suginami Ward, and then a woman's screams were heard: a complaint to this effect was filed at Niiyama Police Box in Yamano, in the same ward. The caller did not dial 110, the police emergency number, but phoned the information straight to the local police box.

The complaint was lodged by Tomiko Fukada (52) of 1-chome Yamano. She supplied her name and address at the time of the call. As head of the women's branch of the local assembly, Tomiko had gotten to know the local police through her participation in neighborhood crime watch initiatives. Senior Patrolman Kazunari Sahashi (55), who answered the call, knew the woman personally and took her report seriously: as soon as he hung up the phone, he pedaled off toward the scene of the alleged disturbance.

The two districts of Yamano and Niikura lay adjacent on an east-west axis. When a new police box was set up between them six years previously, it had been christened "Niiyama," combining the two names. The neighborhoods of 1-chome Yamano and 3-chome Niikura were especially close, separated only by an irrigation canal less than three feet wide, a remnant from the days when the entire vicinity was farmland.

Tomiko Fukada's house fronted on this irrigation canal, and she'd reported that the sounds of quarreling came from a construction site just across the way, where three new houses were going up side by side. Officer Sahashi made a beeline for the site, heading through 1-chome Yamano on a road that went right past the Fukada home. Tomiko was standing outside her front door watching for him, and as he came closer she waved the flashlight in her hand. He drew up and told her to get back inside.

"Right over there, right there!" she said urgently, pointing with the flashlight at a half-built house covered with blue vinyl tarp. It was barely a stone's throw away. "I heard shouting so I looked out the window, and then I heard a woman scream and I saw somebody come out from behind that plastic sheet."

Tomiko Fukada was considerably agitated and apprehensive, so Officer Sahashi instructed her once more to go back indoors and stay there. Then he rode his bicycle across a concrete bridge over the irrigation channel, went up to the blue vinyl tarp covering the half-built houses, and got off.

Yamano and Niikura were residential districts where the rows of houses formed a new and ever-changing townscape that was scarcely distinguishable from any other residential district in the metropolitan area. The traditional landowners were wealthy farmers who had until quite recently been actively promoting agriculture in suburban areas; as a result, relatively fewer tracts of farmland here had been carved up and sold for housing.

That had certainly benefited the community. But around the latter half of the nineties, the burdensome inheritance tax rose to such levels that more and more property owners were forced to sell. In rushed developers and small housing contractors, the former erecting great housing complexes to be sold off in units, the latter throwing up a number of small prefabricated houses, guerrilla-style, and marketing them as "detached houses in the city."

Aerial views of the Yamano–Niikura district had always shown great swaths of green farming land, mixed with smaller patches of residential areas where brightly-hued walls and fences made colorful dots as in a pointillist painting—a rare sort of color map in the metropolitan area. The large green swatches were now disappearing one by one, their space increasingly taken over by small residential quarters. Thanks to the recent sluggish economy, the new dots of color were not clustered as tightly and cohesively as the old. The effect was rather threadbare and lonely.

The three half-finished houses wrapped in blue vinyl sheeting that Officer Sahashi was about to check out corresponded to one tiny dot. The contractor and seller was Yamada Construction, a company known for high prices but also for solidly-built houses. Printed large on the sheeting was the company logo, an outline drawing of a yellow bird constructing a nest on a branch.

As he got off his bike and switched on his flashlight, the first thing that caught Sahashi's eye was that damn bird. If it was nesting in a tree it must be a wild bird, but as far as he could tell, the drawing showed a canary. A bird-watcher in his spare time, Sahashi was irked by this discrepancy every time he went by on patrol. At that moment the familiar protest registered in his mind again, as he later recounted to a colleague, noting that in a crisis situation the brain retained a vivid impression of even tiny details.

The framework of the three houses had just been completed. There was no interim roof; the two-by-four method of construction often used in pre-fabricated houses seldom required one. For that reason, it was essential to wrap the unfinished building securely in vinyl tarp to protect the foundation and pillars from the elements. Yamada Construction was no slouch here, either; he could see at a glance the tarp was firmly in place.

Until its sale to Yamada Construction three years back, this land had been the property of the Eguchis, a wealthy farming family. It was on the small side for a plot of farmland, barely a quarter of an acre in size. The family had retained the pocket of land even after giving up agriculture in the mid-eighties and moving away, since when they had rented it out in twelve-foot-square sections as kitchen gardens. Sahashi had been assigned to this area just when the Niiyama police box was first set up, and he knew all about the rental gardens. Some yielded abundant crops of oddly-shaped but luscious tomatoes and eggplants, while others, perhaps in the hands of novice farmers, had never done well, crop after crop just withering away.

Now, however, over half of the plot lay empty. The three houses under construction occupied one-fourth of a section as rectangular as a chocolate bar, standing isolated in the southwest corner.

Whatever Tomiko Fukada may have seen or heard minutes before, the site was now silent and deserted. Officer Sahashi walked across the dirt, circling the perimeter of the construction site with the beam of his flashlight trained on it. The house on the left end was secure. The center house, secure. The right-end house likewise showed no sign of disturbance.

Sweeping the beam of his flashlight in a circle, he lit up the logo of the little yellow bird once again. As he moved the light from left to right, he noticed something on the tip of a yellow wing. Some sort of drop. He went over for a closer look. There was more than one, he saw. Dark drops, still wet . . . *blood*, he thought.

Until that moment he'd had no intention of pushing back the tarp and venturing inside. Tomiko Fukada may have seen someone coming out of there, but there was no sign of any human presence now. Entering a construction site without due cause could lead to hassles with contractors, even for a cop. If at all possible, he'd rather avoid it.

This was no time for hanging back, though. He gave the tarp a sharp yank, but it was fastened down tight; he could pull it up a foot and a half from the bottom, no more. The contractors had done what they could to keep the site secure. He got down and crawled under as if wriggling his way through a pipe.

No need to look further. The body lay sprawled in plain view. A man in a business suit lay half twisted, his arms bent slightly upward around his face, his legs flung out awkwardly. Next to his head, which was turned on one side, lay a briefcase.

The smell of fresh lumber was overpowered by the coppery smell of blood.

Instinctively laying a hand on his police stick, Sahashi checked his watch. The luminescent hands indicated 10:29 P.M. He shone his flashlight around and picked up a glint six feet or so from the body. Cautiously he went in closer, training his beam on the floor. A knife with a six-inch blade was lying there, the blade and handle smeared with blood. After ascertaining that much, he stepped back to the tarp, crawled outside, and took out his radio.

After reporting the find, he was able to establish an identity in short order using the contents of the victim's briefcase and other effects: Ryosuke Tokoroda, age 48.

There was one other little thing, Officer Sahashi explained later. That neighborhood was really quiet at night. The siren of the patrol car he'd summoned over the wireless must have reached the ears of the victim's family in their house in 2-chome Niikura. The thought was heartbreaking.

3

"Everybody's met everybody, I think," said Shimojima, looking around at each face in turn. Dapper and handsome, the captain had doubtless broken hearts in his day. Turning to Takegami, he asked for word on Naka's condition, his face a picture of concern.

"No change. Which is probably good news, all things considered."

Shimojima gave a series of small nods. "The last thing I want is to lose a member of the team."

"Of course."

Though far from spacious, Chief Tachikawa's office was immaculate; not a speck of dust blemished the desk or even the arms of the sofa provided for visitors. In the open window facing east, and in the framed awards hanging on the walls, the glass sparkled. Chief of Police Tachikawa was a fastidious man. The gold knob topping the Rising Sun flagstaff behind his desk shone, too—no doubt he ordered it polished daily.

"All I can say," said Chief Tachikawa, "is that it's remarkable that Superintendent Kasai approved something this . . . unprecedented."

To Takegami's mind, the chief was not so much worried as scared. His eyes moved restlessly, and his fingertips were fidgety.

Shimojima corrected him mildly. "It's not entirely unprecedented, sir. This approach is by no means unheard of. And even if things don't turn out the way we hope, all we stand to lose is one short afternoon."

"Is that so?"

"Yes. Plus we're dealing with minors here, remember. A more confrontational approach could backfire."

The bold officer and the faint-hearted commander. The words floated unbidden into Takegami's thoughts and he smiled inwardly, listening to the conversation. *Helluva shame Naka's not here to see this. He must have been looking forward to it.*

Lying in his intensive care unit, Naka might be dreaming of this scene even now. His friend's voice seemed to echo in his ears.

—*Dammit all. Sorry, Gami, but you've got to stand in for me. You can do it.*

Noriyoshi Shimojima, although four years Takegami's junior, was head of the Third Squad of the First Criminal Investigation Division of the Tokyo Metropolitan Police Department (MPD). Takegami belonged to the Fourth Squad, so Shimojima's leadership position did not affect him personally. Besides, Takegami was a desk man; this was his first time in donkey's years to be involved in active identification and investigation of suspects.

Desk assignment meant in essence being a paper shuffler. Takegami's main job was churning out the various official documents that detectives needed, single-handed. He also made files of photos, maps, and assorted protocols, and handled the transcription of video and audio tapes. It was a post vital to every criminal investigation; though out of the limelight, the role he played was no minor one.

The task force for a major case involving homicide, grand theft, or kidnapping was drawn from one MPD Criminal Investigation Division squad, combined with detectives from the precinct with jurisdiction over the crime scene. Usually, local precincts did not have anyone trained to cope with the huge load of paperwork that went with a major crime, so the MPD would send someone over. Not just anyone, though. Preparing and submitting official documents was the essence of red-tape bureaucracy, and to anyone not used to it, the job could prove daunting. It was best left for experienced hands. Whether the cop saddled with the job took it as a tribute or a dig, whether he felt trusted or abused, depended on the cop.

There were seven squads in the First Criminal Investigation Division of the MPD, each with its own desk chief. Of the seven pen-pushers, Takegami ranked second in age and length of service. The homicide in the prefab housing construction site in 3-chome Niikura, Suginami Ward, fell under the jurisdiction of Captain Shimojima's Third Squad, whose desk chief was Takegami's lone senior, Fusao Nakamoto. A thirty-year veteran at his post, Nakamoto was someone Takegami valued both as a colleague and as a drinking buddy.

Three days before the 3-chome Niikura incident, sometime after nine on the evening of April twenty-fourth, a college student named Naoko Imai (21) had been strangled at the karaoke club Jewel in Matsumae, Shibuya Ward, where she'd been working part-time; that case fell in the jurisdiction of Takegami's Fourth Squad. At the time, Third Squad was on stand-by (and therefore able to take on the subsequent homicide case in Niikura), leaving Nakamoto with nothing in particular to do, so he'd helped Takegami set up a desk for the task force in the South Shibuya Police Station.

Nakamoto had pitched in not just to be helpful, but for the sake of their shared campaign. He and Takegami were in the midst of negotiations with the brass upstairs to purchase a high-definition scanner for the Division. Like police organizations the world over, the MPD was perennially short-funded; even a requisition for a single new computer meant an enormous hassle. Persuading clueless bigwigs that a scanner would greatly increase the swiftness and accuracy of desk work—and, more to the point, getting them to shell out for one—was harder than selling a rice cooker to an elephant. To the higher echelons, using advanced machinery to reduce people's work-loads was akin to a scam. A detailed report of the working conditions and output of Takegami's new desk operation might help persuade the brass (who needed to be educated about what a "scanner" even was) to heed their request.

Nakamoto explained, "If it was for a case I was handling myself, I could never draw up that kind of a report. Even if I did, they'd assume I doctored the facts and figures to make them come out the way I wanted. I'm telling you, Gami, this is our perfect chance. I'll stay off your toes. Just let me hang around and watch."

Takegami was amenable to the idea. While they were making the arrange-ments, though, the Niikura homicide took place in Suginami Ward and Naka-moto's services were required. Even amid the subsequent storm of paperwork, the two men stayed in touch over the scanner issue. As neither of them was directly involved in the ongoing investigations, they traded no opinions about the development of their respective cases. Still, they shared a clear sense that Takegami's case would drag on while Nakamoto's might wrap up quickly. At this stage, of course, it hadn't occurred to either of them that the two cases could be related.

But two days after the Niikura murder, five days after the murder at Jewel, forensic evidence pointed to a connection. There was not just one strand of linking evidence, either, but several.

First off were the fiber traces found on the victims' clothing. The material was an unremarkable synthetic, but its hue was unusual, coming from a blue dyestuff not manufactured domestically—or in China, Taiwan, South Korea, or any other Asian country. Close analysis revealed it to be a chemical dye made exclusively by a manufacturing company in Ottawa, Canada, during the brief interval from December 1998 through March 1999. It had been special-ordered by an Ottawa apparel company.

The apparel company had used chemical fibers dyed bright blue with this dyestuff to make two different clothing items, a vest and a parka. Both were popular, standard-issue items; this particular color, christened "millennium blue," was used in limited editions of two hundred each to be marketed, in line with the color name, as Christmas presents for the year 1999. The bulk of the shipment sold out. The numbers were so small that none had entered Japan except for a few personal imports. Still, a TV celebrity had worn one on a Christmas Eve program, so among the younger generation the shade millennium blue was well known.

Identical samples of this scarce clothing fiber had been found on the bodies of Naoko Imai and Ryosuke Tokoroda. Only trace amounts were detected, suggesting that in both cases the assailant had been wearing the article of clothing at the time of the attack, with fibers from it adhering to the victim during the ensuing struggle. Hearing that the vest and parka were made in Canada, Takegami had pictured arctic wear appropriate for mountaineering, but they had turned out to be ordinary street wear. Even this late in April, Tokyo temperatures often plummeted after sundown. It was no surprise that the murderer should have dressed warmly.

There was other overlapping physical evidence as well.

Naoko Imai's murder had taken place not inside one of the private booths in the karaoke club Jewel, but on the emergency stairs off the fourth floor. The ground floor of the eight-floor building was a restaurant; Jewel occupied the second, third, and fourth floors, with the reception on the second. Customers had no occasion to take the emergency stairs, but staff used them to slip easily back and forth. The connecting doors were not sealed off, so anybody with a mind to go through them could easily have done so—otherwise the stairs would, of course, be useless in an emergency.

On the night of the deadly assault, interior finishing work was being done just above the fourth floor, and workers had been using the emergency stairs; they were discouraged from using the elevator in work clothes during business hours, to avoid setting off howls of protest from the other tenants. The white paint they were using had dripped and spattered copiously all over the stairs, protective sheeting hung up to prevent this very thing from happening proving sadly inadequate to the task. Here and there, the outline of a paint-can bottom showed clear as day.

Naoko Imai's assailant had stepped in this paint and gotten it on the bottoms of his or her shoes, the arcs of the heels making clear white imprints on the linoleum stairs. The rest of the footprint was unfortunately invisible, making it impossible to tell the shoe shape or size. However, trace amounts of identical white paint had been detected in the ground alongside the body of Ryosuke Tokoroda. White paint by that manufacturer was not being used at the construction site, nor did any appear on the soles of Tokoroda's shoes. There could be only one explanation: his killer's shoes were flecked with the paint being used at Jewel.

At this point, Nakamoto and Takegami agreed it wouldn't be long before the two investigations merged and they were working in tandem after all. Nakamoto predicted that his smaller team, the one from Suginami, would be the one to make the move.

While the bosses weighed what to do, another set of telling facts emerged. Three years earlier, when Naoko Imai was a second-year student at a private high school called Sakurada Girls' Academy, she had worked part-time as food monitor for the main office of Orion Foods, where Ryosuke Tokoroda was employed. Not only that, Tokoroda had headed the advertising team that recruited high-school girls to sample a new food supplement then under development. It thus seemed likely that the two victims had been acquainted.

But Tokoroda's boss and colleagues had no recollection of Naoko Imai.

Her name aroused the faintest of reactions, and her photograph met with shrugs. As one put it, "Look, we only needed ten high school girls, and a good eighty to a hundred must've applied. Sure, we had them all show their student IDs, and we kept records, but who's gonna remember all those names and faces?"

Besides, around age twenty is when a young woman's appearance changes the most. Without the company's part-time hiring records, the connection between the two murder victims would not have been at all easy to ferret out.

In the end, seven days after Ryosuke Tokoroda's death, the two investigations did merge. As Nakamoto had predicted, the Suginami team moved to South Shibuya.

A reshuffling of roles now took place. Command of the on-site investigations went to Captain Shimojima of the Third Squad in place of Captain Kamiya on Takegami's Fourth Squad, who graciously ceded control of his South Shibuya team. Shimojima returned the compliment by letting on that his outfit had called on the other for aid. Takegami thought how typical it was of Kamiya not to get hung up at a time like this on attempts to save face.

Takegami and Nakamoto went on performing their desk jobs with quiet efficiency, keeping their hopes for a scanner to themselves. They took advantage of the opportunity to put their heads together and experiment with new ways of handling the work.

The resolution of a case is sometimes likened to the Biblical account of the parting of the Red Sea, as if one day all the mysteries suddenly melt away like the swirling waters of chaos, dividing neatly to reveal a dry path. It was nothing like that, Takegami thought. Calling unsolved cases "labyrinthine," though, was right on the money. No map, just Ariadnes on all sides, each holding out a different thread. Short of walking around and exploring for yourself, there was no way to tell which one might lead to the correct solution. In the end, all you could do was trudge on, searching high and low. Even if someone handed the beleaguered investigation team a staff of Moses, one that could split the labyrinth right down the middle, they'd likely just lean on it to rest their aching feet before getting on with the hunt.

Had there been a personal connection between Ryosuke Tokoroda and

Naoko Imai? That was the crucial question. From the start, the investigating team poured energy into finding out.

Naoko Imai's part-time job with Orion Foods had involved monitoring a food supplement then being marketed by the company, and answering questions about her eating habits. The job had lasted three months, but since the subjects' responses were recorded on paper and over the phone, face-to-face contact between the monitors and the Orion Foods staff had been limited to the initial explanatory meeting. Also, since Ryosuke Tokoroda was in charge of organizing the results of the project, he'd never had direct dealings with any of the girls about their reports. Several other people had handled that, all of them female employees and none of them connected directly to him.

Fortunately, the woman who'd been in charge of receiving Naoko Imai's reports remembered her quite well. Cheerful and lively and a big talker, unwilling to hang up even after she'd filed her report; listening to the girl run on had been interesting in a way, she said, but also a bit of a pain— which was why she stuck in her mind.

At the time, the woman staffer herself had been a freshman employee, and being assigned to the advertising team with no preparation had made it difficult to adapt to the work environment. Dealing with the high school girls was a relief, as they were close to her in age, but when she let down her guard with them they sometimes took advantage of her, mouthing off or missing their deadlines. That made her mad, she admitted to the detective assigned to interview her.

"Naoko Imai wasn't spoiled that way, but she did like to chitchat about fashion and cosmetics and so on. And she seemed interested in what life was like for somebody like me, an office worker new on the job. She asked me once what my salary was. She said after she got out of college, she wanted to work for a big company, too, if she could. When I asked if she had any specific kind of work in mind, she said as long as the pay was good and there were plenty of cute, go-getter guys around, almost anything would do. I had to laugh. She was so upfront about it, so down-to-earth."

Then the woman casually let drop something that gave the investigators pause.

"Orion Foods isn't a very big food company, but we do have a name for ourselves. Which might be why Naoko applied for the part-time job with us in the first place. She asked me all about the employment test and so on. And she kept going on about the men she'd met at the briefing, how good-looking they were. 'If there's ever a company mixer, you make sure I get invited, now,' she'd joke. I never responded to any of that, but it didn't seem like a total joke; I got the definite idea she was interested in the men on the team. She mentioned she liked older men because they were so dependable. I never took her for one of those young girls who date older men for money, mind you, but I did get the idea that she was on the look-out for a boyfriend—preferably someone mature, with deep pockets."

Having said that, she emphasized, "Still, I never once heard her say Mr. Tokoroda's name. As far as I know, she had no contact with him, ever. This is all just in my head. But I have to say, Mr. Tokoroda was in charge of the team, and he was the oldest member; everybody else was young, women included. So when Naoko Imai went on about good-looking men it's possible that the face she had in mind belonged to Mr. Tokoroda. Whether he knew it or not, I really couldn't say."

Meanwhile, Naoko Imai's friends reported that for a while she'd gone around telling everyone she was having an affair with an older man—a married man, no less. That had been around the end of her second year in high school and the start of her third and final year, some six months after the part-time job with Orion Foods. By the summer, she'd let on that the affair was not going well, and before long had taken up with a new boyfriend.

Had Naoko Imai's partner in that illicit affair—an affair that seemed a curious blend of decidedly modern, unsentimental views on "hooking up" and unrealistic, girlishly romantic dreams—been Ryosuke Tokoroda? Her work as monitor might not have brought them into direct contact, but given her interest in him, if she had ever run into him in the neighborhood or caught sight of him at the train station, she could easily have struck up a conversation. The main offices of Orion Foods were adjacent to her high school, and the same train station was handy to each of them. It wasn't impossible. It even looked like a good bet that the two victims had been on close terms—

And then, another Ariadne came on the scene.

She was not a minor, but somewhat ironically the detectives took to calling her "Miss A," as if she were a juvenile offender whose identity was protected under law. Miss A was definitely a prime suspect. But without hard evidence, they were unable to implicate her publicly by name.

Miss A was a member of Naoko Imai's seminar class. Having taken a year off between high school and college to retake the highly competitive university entrance exams, she was a year older. A serious student, she earned good grades, and her acquaintances spoke highly of her. Her hometown was far away, so like most out-of-town students she took a studio apartment and managed to get by on a small monthly allowance. That meant inconspicuous clothes and a simple lifestyle—just the opposite of Naoko Imai.

To use an old-fashioned expression, Naoko Imai and Miss A had been rivals in love. Naoko's most recent boyfriend, a college student who'd showed up at the funeral and been IDed by the police, had previously dated Miss A. In fact he and Miss A had gone together ever since entering college, and had been recognized as a couple by their friends.

Then Naoko Imai had come along and snatched the boyfriend right out from under Miss A's nose. That was some six months ago. Naturally, Miss A was left feeling hurt and angry. It's the sort of little tragedy that happens all the time, one that everybody experiences at least once in a lifetime—none of which makes it any easier. There had been some intense scenes between the three of them. That too was common knowledge in their circle of friends.

In the end, it always comes down to the same thing: abandoned lovers cannot prevail. Instead of clinging to a lost cause, the only sensible thing for Miss A to do was to get on with her life—but to one so serious and pure in heart, the boyfriend's betrayal was unforgivable. And she could not let him go. Time after time she ran tilting at him like Don Quixote, but always with the same result: he rejected her and fled in annoyance, while Naoko Imai laughed in disdain.

Miss A also apparently took offense at Naoko Imai's "immoral" conduct. The name Ryosuke Tokoroda never came out, but it was common knowledge that she had carried on an affair with a married man. Naoko herself had talked openly about it, so of course everyone knew. Miss A was probably stunned to think she'd been replaced in her sweetheart's affections by someone who plunged into illicit sexual relationships without remorse, advertised the fact, and spent all her time thinking about men and clothes without taking her studies seriously. Takegami could imagine Miss A's dismay. If he were her faculty advisor, he thought, he'd sit her down and lecture her that the world is basically unfair, and when it comes to male–female relationships, no rules of logic apply.

Miss A had made no secret of her feelings, telling anyone who would listen that she could kill Naoko Imai, that she would never forgive her boyfriend for betraying her, that she would make him pay if it was the last thing she did. All of which she freely admitted. In fact, right after Naoko Imai's murder, it had been the talk of their seminar class that she might be the killer. Knowing that suspicion rested on her, she had felt like she was sitting on a bed of nails.

At the investigation headquarters at South Shibuya Police Station, a decision was made to take a detailed statement from Miss A. Just as they were on the point of doing so, first Ryosuke Tokoroda was killed, and then the links between the two killings came to light. Miss A had held a grudge against Naoko Imai all right, but Tokoroda apparently had meant nothing to her. What were the police to make of it?

The answer came, surprisingly, from Miss A herself. The day after the two investigations merged, she arrived at the police station accompanied by her mother, who made a special trip to Tokyo for the occasion, and volunteered her story. (Several newspapers got wind of this and, misunderstanding, published erroneous reports of the killer's apprehension. Nakamoto gleefully cut them out. Collecting samples of published misinformation on criminal investigations was a pet hobby of his.)

Miss A spoke quietly and collectedly to the detective assigned to take down her statement.

"As a matter of fact, I did meet Mr. Tokoroda. One time only. He sat in once when I had a talk with Naoko Imai. She brought him along. She said it would be a good idea to have an adult listen in."

It had been a Sunday afternoon, just after New Year, she said. She kept a diary faithfully, and knew the exact place and time.

"It was in a coffee shop near Shibuya Station. I'd say we were there from about two to four. The place is a little off the main stretch, hard to find, so it was almost empty. Naoko and Mr. Tokoroda were already there when I arrived."

Ryosuke Tokoroda had introduced himself to Miss A as an acquaintance of Naoko Imai, "something like an older brother." She explained, "This was the fourth or fifth time I'd hashed things out with Naoko. Sometimes it was just the two of us, and sometimes . . . my ex-boyfriend was there. But this was the only time Mr. Tokoroda ever showed up."

Miss A claimed that Naoko Imai had behaved around Mr. Tokoroda with an easy familiarity, and that he had responded in kind. "She had her arm through his and she kept, you know, hanging on him. He just sat there and let her, the whole time he was lecturing me. He said I couldn't go around resenting people just because I'd had a messy breakup. He said my boyfriend probably got tired of me because I dwell on things too much and let them get me down. He said it was time to stop acting so childish. Naoko sat there grinning away, and that drove me crazy. So I went ahead and told him—

"'You say you're here as a kind of older brother. Fair enough, but did you know she came right out and told her boyfriend she'd had an affair with a man your age? She practically *bragged* about it. What do you say to that?'"

Naoko Imai had dissolved in giggles. "'What are you talking about?' she said. 'Does he *know*? This is the guy! He's the one I was telling you about! We don't sleep together anymore, but we're still friends. That's why he's here, to support me.'"

She'd been too appalled to say anything, Miss A told the detective. "Mr. Tokoroda did look unhappy. Anyway, after that I decided there was no use trying to talk sense into either of them, so I got up and walked out the door. Naoko just kept on laughing, but Mr. Tokoroda came running out after me."

And offered her a sincere apology, she said. "He said she was always like that, and he didn't know what to do with her, but that he felt like he had to do *something*. He told me I should stay away from her, but that if he could help me in any way he'd be happy to. I should feel free to talk to him any time. He handed me his business card. I didn't want it, but he practically forced me to take it. I took off as fast as I could then, heading for the station. While I was waiting for the train, I checked out the card. It had the name of his company on it, Orion Foods, and on the back he'd written his email address and cell phone number. After that, I was so . . . mortified, and sad, and I don't know what . . . I just went straight home. But I kept turning it over and over in my mind . . ."

Asked why she was offering these compromising details, Miss A replied, "After what happened to Naoko, I knew the police would think it was me. I figured they'd have no choice. But I didn't kill her. No way. Since I didn't do it, the idea of being investigated didn't bother me. I was sure it was just a matter of time till the truth came out . . . But then when Mr. Tokoroda got killed, and they established a connection between that and Naoko's murder, and word started going round that it was a serial murder, I freaked. It was almost like somebody was deliberately setting me up. After all, I knew both of the victims. Once the police figured that out—and once they knew *how* I knew them—I was afraid they'd be more convinced than ever that I did it. And then I could say I was innocent till I was blue in the face, for all the good *that* would do me.

"So at first I thought I'd keep it to myself about knowing Mr. Tokoroda, because if I didn't let on, who would ever know? But then people started carrying on about how it was a serial killer, and I couldn't stand it anymore. Because maybe a waiter or somebody in that coffee shop had seen me with him there. And maybe they'd remember, and tell the police. How could I defend myself then? I'd look bad for sure, and I was afraid the next thing I knew, the police would be pinning the murders on me. That's why I decided to come in and tell you about it myself. Because I'm not the one you want. I didn't kill those two. I haven't got anything to feel guilty about."

She lived alone and had no alibi for either of the murders. She'd been alone at home on both occasions, she said, and hadn't spoken to anyone on the telephone, so there was nothing to back her up. On the other hand, no eyewitness testimony placed her anywhere near either crime scene, and no traces of white paint were found on the soles of the shoes she willingly turned over for examination. Lacking evidence for a search warrant, forensics couldn't look for blue fibers, but neither had anyone testified to seeing her in a vest or parka of that shade—a startlingly bright blue, not easily forgotten—prior to the murders. She hadn't been to North America recently, and no one had testified to giving or lending her any apparel of millennium blue. There was no solid material evidence whatsoever, just a jumble of incriminating impressions.

Evidence from the murder methods was no more helpful. Naoko Imai had been strangled, but not with anyone's bare hands. Someone had put vinyl rope or something similar around her neck from behind, and pulled it tight; there were well-defined marks on the nape where the two lines of rope had crossed. Also, just below the right shoulder blade was a fist-sized area of congested blood—a distinctive bruise typically caused by an assailant laying the victim prone and holding him or her down forcibly by digging in a knee. With the advantage of surprise, a woman might well use this method to commit murder. Imai, a perpetual dieter, had been relatively frail and weak, but Miss A was tall and had been on her high school volleyball team, giving her superior strength (as she was first to admit). She could easily have done it. But of course it would have been still easier for a man; the fact that a woman *could* have carried out the murder proved nothing in itself.

Ryosuke Tokoroda's case was more complicated. The murder weapon was a six-inch kitchen knife abandoned at the scene of the crime, but so common a type that it could not be traced. There was no kitchen knife in Miss A's apartment. She didn't own one, she said; apparently she did her own cooking but never fixed anything fancy.

Tokoroda had exhibited twenty-four stab wounds all over his body. The cause of death was shock from loss of blood. Eight of the wounds were potentially fatal; the other sixteen were shallower, occurring with apparent randomness on the tip of the shoulder, the side, the kneecap, the shin, and elsewhere. Judging from defensive wounds on the arms and palms, the victim had at first stood face-to-face with his assailant, who came at him straight on; as he crumpled over to protect the wound area he was pushed over on his back, then stabbed repeatedly as he lay supine. The killer had likely sat astride him. All twenty-four wounds showed vital reactions, indicating that the victim had been alive at the time they were inflicted. However, judging from the angle and degree of twist, as well as calculations showing which way the blade had been turned, approximately half were inflicted after Tokoroda lost consciousness and ceased to put up a fight.

Stabbing somebody face-to-face takes guts. Even if you're armed for the confrontation, when the time comes for action it's no easy matter to follow through. However, a flare-up of temper can cause a rush of blood to the head and a breakdown in talking, making it easier to get carried away and cross that first line, excitement piling on excitement in a mounting frenzy while you stab, again and again—till suddenly you look down and see the other person lying mutilated in a pool of blood. That is the all-too common pattern in stabbing homicides. Surprisingly little muscle power is called for, as adrenaline does the rest. Petite women have been known to wield a kitchen knife with enough force to sever a man's rib. Everything depends on the circumstances; therefore, the modus operandi alone is not a good predictor of a murderer's gender.

Forensic examination of the twenty-four stab wounds led to speculation that they were not all inflicted by the same person. The simultaneous existence of deep, potentially fatal wounds and a great many shallow wounds—some barely more than scratches—suggested that several people of different physical strength and intensity may have participated in the crime.

The first time he filed that report, Takegami was put in mind of a famous mystery novel from overseas involving multiple assailants, and mentioned it to Nakamoto.

There was another possibility, however. The forensic report went on to note that while the deepest wounds included some inflicted at the onset of the crime (when the victim was still upright), the shallower ones were all made as he lay flat on his back. This suggested that a single individual might have lost wind and tired in the course of inflicting so many stab wounds, losing strength until no longer able to take steady aim. Again, this scenario was of no help in determining the sex of the offender.

Amidst all this speculation stood Miss A, shakily, as their prime suspect. The case against her was tenuous indeed. Motive she had in spades—at least as far as Naoko Imai went. But what about Ryosuke Tokoroda? Assuming she'd acted alone, after the Imai murder she would already have been feeling the brunt of suspicion; to kill Tokoroda so soon afterward would have taken a powerful motive, but there wasn't any.

Or was there? According to Miss A's testimony, Tokoroda had demonstrated excessive interest in her affairs, like a meddling snoop. Suppose that after Imai's murder, as suspicion came to rest on Miss A, he'd gotten in touch with her somehow and offered to be of assistance; suppose he'd told her that if she was guilty, the best thing to do was turn herself in; suppose he'd then met her face to face near the scene of the crime in Niikura and said something fatally ruinous to her self-respect, winding up dead himself; wasn't that a possible scenario? It could well have happened that way.

Eyewitness Tomiko Fukada had testified to hearing a woman's scream that night. Whether there'd been one killer or more, a woman had definitely been at the site. But who? Was it fair to assume it had been Miss A, and focus only on her?

Proof, that's all they needed. Positive eyewitness testimony. There was no way they could let someone with this much motive just walk away. That was the consensus of the joint investigation team.

But then one day—about two weeks after the Niikura homicide, as Takegami recalled—Nakamoto took the unusual step of offering his own opinion on the case.

Takegami was surprised. Not just that Nakamoto would air a personal theory, although that was surprising enough. What amazed him was that at a strategy session that same day he'd just watched several young detectives set forth practically the same theory, only to be given short shrift. They were still smarting from the experience, and angry.

The detectives had suggested setting aside the theory that Miss A was the perp, and focusing on some other person's involvement with the victims. Miss A was their number one suspect only because they were taking Naoko Imai as the starting point. If they tried digging around a little in Ryosuke Tokoroda's life, they might come up with a completely different motive.

"Naka, let me guess. You heard those guys complaining."

Nakamoto laughed, smoothing the thinning hair on the top of his head. "Unlike present company, I don't pay much attention to what youngsters say. Still, it goes to show I'm not the only one who had the idea." He did not look at all displeased. "Looks like the old guy still has what it takes, eh? For more than desk work, I mean . . . not that there's anything wrong with desk work."

"I know what you mean." Takegami nodded.

But Nakamoto clamped his mouth shut. He looked ill at ease. More than what he'd said, the guilty look on his face after that hastily tacked-on disclaimer struck Takegami as coming from the heart.

Could be Nakamoto's tired of his desk job, he thought. Even a man that devoted to his career, whose work was universally admired and relied on, came to the point where he'd had enough, where he was burned-out. What about himself? For ten seconds Takegami thought it over, hand on chest.

Several days went by with no new information regarding Miss A and no new discoveries of any kind, despite thorough digging. The investigators' mood was glum. The young cops brought forward their theory again, and again it was shunted aside.

Nakamoto was sunk in thought, and strangely fidgety. As he and Takegami enjoyed a lunch of buckwheat noodles together one day, he blurted out, as if the thought had just come to him, "This is out of character for me, granted, but after thirty years on the job, I'm thinking of doing something besides desk work."

"What, submit a recommendation?"

"Nothing so formal," he said with a laugh and a wave of his hand. "I'll just have a word or two with Captain Shimojima."

Thirty years on the job. The words carried weight. He'd said them as if realizing only now just how long he'd been in the shadows.

Takegami did not try to stop him. Remembering what had happened the other day, he read his friend's mind and said nothing; besides, he figured nothing he could say would dissuade him. He was inclined to make light of the situation.

But with surprising swiftness, Nakamoto's plan was approved for immediate action. Takegami was flabbergasted.

"Actually, Shimojima said he'd been thinking the same thing, but the atmosphere at the meetings was too negative. He was figuring he'd have to be the one to pull the pin on the grenade. Fools rush in," Naka added with a self-deprecating laugh—but he looked happy.

After that, it was a matter of hunkering down and working out the details. Nakamoto left his desk, Takegami stayed put. Nakamoto sketched it all in for him, though, and he had to admit the plan was well thought out. Hearing Shimojima was officially calling it "merely one arm of the ongoing investigation," Takegami smiled to himself. The guy was covering his ass.

The plan called for a policewoman, so headquarters hurriedly sent to Suginami Station for one. When he heard it was to be Chikako Ishizu, Takegami was again caught off balance. This case was full of surprises.

Chikako Ishizu. Now there was a familiar name. But before he could let himself indulge in fond memories, he couldn't help grimacing. The woman had gotten herself in a pile of shit. Four years back, as part of the MPD arson team, during the investigation of a serial homicide case that had taken an unexpected twist she'd disobeyed a direct order and as a result had been demoted—left out in the cold. With her name in the mud, they couldn't even send her to the PR Division. *Suginami*, thought Takegami. *So that's where she ended up.*

Of course Nakamoto too knew all about Chikako Ishizu and her "misconduct." Lowering his voice, he cupped a hand around his mouth and whispered, "You know, that Shimojima's a cagey bastard. If anything goes wrong, what do you bet he's planning to pin the blame on her?"

Probably a good guess, Takegami thought. Out loud he said, "You should be more worried about yourself."

"Nah, I'm okay. The worst that could happen is that I go back to my desk. I haven't got long till retirement anyway."

"Maybe you're right at that."

"Yeah." For a second, as if to catch a glimpse of something passing swiftly by, Nakamoto narrowed his eyes. Then he said, "If it means getting back on the front line, then even if I have to tread on a minefield, it's okay by me."

Takegami nodded silently back at him. Just maybe, not too far in the future he too would tire of being a desk jockey and long for a place in the sun. Maybe he'd itch to feel the satisfaction of knowing he'd cracked a case. Stranger things had happened. Knowing that, he nodded.

—And yet.

Even if he could relax about Nakamoto, there remained the matter of Chikako Ishizu. He worried about her. He was in no position to be of any real support, but he vowed to himself that he would keep a watchful eye on her.

But hey—no point in being pessimistic. It might just work out that Naka-moto and she got credit for a job well done. What Nakamoto was capable of remained to be seen, but Chikako was no slouch, he knew. Besides, with her motherly temperament she was ideally suited to the role they were handing her.

And so the preparations were made and everything was ready to go, with nothing left to do but wait for the big day.

Then, suddenly, Nakamoto collapsed.

He had a myocardial infarction. This was not the first time. Before, it had been mild—a little chest pain, nothing more—and he'd been released from the hospital right away. This time it was different. He fell down unconscious while climbing the stairs in the station, and was whisked away to the hospi-tal by ambulance without ever coming to.

That had been the day before yesterday, in the afternoon. Today he was still in a coma in the ICU, his condition critical. But implementation of the plan he had conceived and helped develop could not be postponed. Shimo-jima was utterly incapable of standing in for him; Superintendent Kasai would never approve. Who would take over the central role Nakamoto had been scheduled to play?

Shimojima had decided to use Nakamoto so that if the plan failed, it would be easy to make excuses. With nobody from the front line of the investigation involved, any mishaps would be easy to cover up. In fact, only a handful of the task force members were fully apprised of the plan. Most were paying no attention.

However, Captain Kamiya of the Fourth Squad was no fool, and he knew his desk chief inside and out. As soon as the furor over Nakamoto's hospital-ization had somewhat died down, he summoned Takegami to the hall outside the briefing room and asked him point-blank, "Gami, are you going to volunteer as Nakamoto's stand-in?"

Takegami gave him a wry smile. "Well, who else is there?"

"Chikako Ishizu could do it. She was on board anyway. She'd just be switching from a supporting role to the lead. Anyway, she's got nothing to lose."

Before Takegami could ask if he was serious, Kamiya burst out laughing. "I'm joking."

"Right. I figured." Takegami laughed back.

"You know what I think? Naka must have been fed up with desk work. He must have wanted to get back in action." *So Kamiya picked up on that, too.* "Otherwise, he'd just have given us his idea, and left it to someone else to carry out. That's what you'd have done, Gami, right?"

"I'm not fed up with my job. I like it. It's an interesting job."

Captain Kamiya did not banter. He grunted with approval.

"Gami, you'd do this even if I told you not to, wouldn't you?"

"I would not. Not without your permission, sir. It's not my place to do that."

"I'm not stopping you. Go on. You have my permission."

He set off down the hall, tossing back over his shoulder, "Don't worry, it'll all be over in a few hours. If you pull it off, great, and if not, no harm done." Then he added with conviction, "I have a gut feeling this'll work."

"Thank you." Takegami bowed his head.

As he entered the briefing room, he sought out Shimojima's face. Seeing the captain's clear relief at his offer, his thoughts turned again to his friend *Okay, Naka. Here goes nothing.*

And that's how Takegami came to be where he was now, a last-minute stand-in for the lead role of their little drama. Would he fluff his lines?

From: Mom
To: Minoru
Subject: The new house

Did Dad tell you about the new house? He says he wants a study. The house now is an old one that was remodeled, and apparently it's starting to show its age.

There are some attractive homes going up in the neighborhood, but they'd be farther from the station, so he's debating what to do. He says the secret of buying property is to go there more than once or twice. You have to go back again and again, he says, seeing it in different weather conditions and at different times of the day. Apparently he stops off there on his way home from work. Isn't that nice! I'd love for him to take me along the next time he goes. Do you suppose that'd be asking too much?

4

"We'll use Interrogation Room Two. It's a bit cramped, but that doesn't matter," said Chikako Ishizu, leading the way downstairs. Takegami and Detective Tokunaga followed behind her, carrying the investigation files. "The windows in Room One face north and east, so it's gloomy in the afternoon."

"Besides, the two-way mirror in Room Two is brand-new. They just replaced it last month," Tokunaga chimed in, pulling abreast of Takegami. "I heard somebody hurled a chair at the old one and smashed it to pieces. I wonder which case that was."

Interrogation Room Two lay at the end of a winding corridor. The Shibuya Police Station was not old; however, the lighting was so bad that the interior was dim throughout. The neon letters over the emergency exit at the end of the corridor shone bright even in daytime.

Seated on the bench outside Room Two was a big man—Fourth Squad's Shingo Akizu, a young detective on good terms with Takegami. Seeing the trio arrive, he got up with a smirk. Tucked under his right arm was a bundle of rolled-up papers.

"I got the rundown. Fun and games, huh?"

"Fun? Don't be too sure."

"Lighten up, Gami. Hey, Tokumatsu."

At the nickname, Tokunaga made a face. He despised his given name, "Matsuo," written with characters for "pine tree" and "man"; its slightly old-fashioned ring jarred with his cool, man-about-town persona. Akizu was ragging him deliberately.

"Sure you aren't off to Orion Foods?" he shot back. "I heard you saying how hot their receptionist is."

"Not my type. Looks alone don't do it for me. She's too small. I like 'em long and tall. She'd be perfect for you, though, Tokumatsu. I can just see the two of you—you know, like one of those itty-bitty doll sets made of quail eggs."

Akizu was over six feet tall, while Tokunaga was about five foot five. His height—or lack of it—was another sore point with the man about town. It was Akizu's annoying habit to make fun of whatever people were most self-conscious about.

Takegami waved him off.

"All right, fellas, let's not stand around chewing the fat," said Chikako with a smile, pushing open the door to Room Two.

Akizu introduced himself genially. "Chikako Ishizu, isn't it? I'm Shingo Akizu, Gami's protégé."

"Funny, I don't remember taking you on," commented Takegami. "Since when did you decide to put in for a desk job?"

"If I did, would you take me on?"

"Not a chance. Scatterbrains can't hack it."

"Whoa." Akizu took the roll of papers in his right hand and hit himself on the head in mock self-condemnation. "Pardon *me*. Actually," he went on, "all I wanted was the pleasure of meeting Gami-san's dream girl from his younger days. Right, Detective Ishizu?"

Chikako's eyes widened. "You mean me?"

"Who else?"

Takegami cut in. "Tokunaga, go get a broom and sweep this big lummox outa here." He slipped past Chikako and stepped inside the room. "Don't waste your time talking to a dumb-ass like him."

"Hear that, Dumb-Ass?" said Tokunaga, puffing out his chest. "Detective Ishizu, is there a broom over there you could hand me?"

"Sure you're man enough to sweep me up, Quail-Butt?" Akizu turned his attention back to Chikako. "When you get some time I hope you'll sit down and tell me what it was like working with Gami back when. I'd be very interested to hear."

"Fine by me. If you want to listen to an old lady's reminiscences."

"I'll be looking forward to it. See ya, Quail. Don't flutter around and get in Gami's way, now, hear?" Akizu strode off down the corridor, leaving Tokunaga fuming until, urged by Chikako, he finally stepped inside the interrogation room.

Takegami was standing at the window with his arms folded, looking out through the sturdy bars. Directly below was the station parking lot; on the other side of a narrow one-way street was a squalid cluster of houses, tenant buildings and condos. A thin layer of white cloud covered the blue sky, and a spring breeze brought distant echoes of Shibuya traffic.

Takegami turned around. The wall to his left was solid, but the one on his right contained a built-in two-way mirror. He went over and stroked it, for no particular reason.

In the center of the room was a single desk flanked by two metal chairs across from each other. There was another small table by the window, where the policeman assigned the job of record-keeping sat. The room was otherwise bare except for a wall interphone. It looked like your typical police interrogation room as seen on TV dramas. All that was missing was a lamp to shine in the suspect's face, and a cheap metal ashtray.

Takegami pulled out a chair and sat down. The chair scraped harshly against the floor.

"How many years has it been for you?" asked Chikako. She was standing with her back to the door.

"Well . . . I wonder. A good ten, anyway, since I did anything like this."

"So you were assigned to desk work right away."

"I don't dislike it, you know."

Tokunaga went over to the desk by the window and spread out the forms he'd been holding under his arm. "I've done this before," he said.

"So I heard," said Takegami.

"I'll just carry on as usual, shall I?"

"That's the idea."

"Okay. Just wanted to make sure. Don't you need an ashtray?"

"Not right away. Let's save it to bring out later, in case we need to stall for time."

"Very good," said Tokunaga with a graceful wave of his hand. No wonder a bumpkin like Akizu found him such an easy target.

As if on the same wavelength, Takegami and Chikako simultaneously checked their watches. 2:10 P.M.

"Well," said Chikako, "it's about time I went down to the lobby."

"Yes, go ahead. Will she be coming alone?"

"No, with her mother. I'll ask the mother to wait in another room."

Takegami nodded. "Probably a good idea. But if the girl insists on having her mother with her, you can bring her along."

"I don't think that will happen."

Catching the implication of her words, Takegami glanced at Chikako inquisitively. She nodded.

"Harue Tokoroda and Kazumi aren't at all close. Kazumi wanted to come alone today; her mother's only here because she was dead set on coming along. Kazumi thinks her mother is an interfering busybody. Probably a typical adolescent phase."

"My daughter's treated me like a pain in the neck ever since she was ten. When she was still in grade school, I'd come home sometimes and she'd say, 'Daddy, are you going to spend the night here?' You'd have thought she wanted me to pay up my bill."

Chikako and Tokunaga laughed. Tokunaga said, "Captain Shimojima was saying the same thing about his kid."

Chikako asked Takegami, "Has your daughter turned twenty yet?"

"Yeah, she had her coming-of-age party last year. She's a junior in college now. Thinks she knows everything."

After marveling that his daughter could be so grown up, and expressing her fondness for the little girl she remembered, Chikako left the room. Takegami spread out his papers, took out a pair of glasses from his breast pocket, and set them on the bridge of his nose.

Tokunaga said in surprise, "You use reading glasses?"

"I picked up a ready-made pair yesterday."

"You really should have your vision tested, and get a pair specially made."

"I don't actually need them."

Seeing Tokunaga chuckle, Takegami hastily added, "No, really. I'm not being defensive. My eyes are fine. I just thought it might be better if I wore glasses today."

Tokunaga thought a moment, and then asked, "To keep her from seeing through you?"

"Something like that."

"I don't think you have anything to worry about."

"Hope you're right."

The phone rang.

"She's here," said Takegami.

From: Kazumi
To: Minoru
Subject: i hate myself

i don't understand anything and i'm sick of trying. what's
wrong with me?

minoru aren't you worried at all? i worry about anything
and everything. like does anybody need me? love me?
sometimes i feel so out of it. i feel like i'm a total
mess. if i disappeared would my friends even miss me?
they'd just find a new friend and forget about the old.
it's the same for you isn't it? parents are no better.
they say your parents are the only ones who love you
unconditionally but that's total crap. who'd want a kid
that turned out bad? it'd be better to have no kid at all.
i'm nothing like what they must have wanted.

i bet they ask themselves what they ever did to deserve a
daughter like me.

From: Dad
To: Kazumi
Subject: Don't worry

Minoru asked me to say something to you because you worry
about things too much. Kazumi, your mother and I love you,
and we're proud of you. You are a great kid.

5

When Kazumi Tokoroda walked into the South Shibuya Police Station, several young men standing in the lobby watched with interest, their heads turning in unison as if pulled by a string. Kazumi ignored them. Not because she was too distracted by fear or nervousness to see them. See them she did, and sent an unambiguous signal that they had no right to be ogling her.

In stark contrast to her daughter's aplomb, Harue Tokoroda was unmistakably frightened. Her eyes darted about the room. She looked every person in the eye, one by one, as if she felt it necessary to explain what she and her daughter were doing in such a place. She looked pitiful.

Mother and daughter differed strikingly in their style of dress, too. Harue was wearing a knit suit of charcoal gray, with a simple black leather handbag and matching shoes. Apart from her wedding ring, she wore no accessories. Kazumi, on the other hand, was wearing a half-sleeve cut-and-sew top and a miniskirt that showed a good eight inches of thigh. Her bare legs were long and slim, and on her feet she wore mules. Her skirt was black, made of some shiny material; the top had a geometric pattern in black and white. Between her shapely breasts swung a silver cross, dangling from an elaborate chain. Her hair was bleached to chestnut, and she wore it shoulder length, tucked back behind one ear to reveal a tiny gold pierced earring.

Even back in Chikako's day, some college students had dressed like this. But sixteen- and seventeen-year-olds this fashion-conscious had generally tended to be delinquents. Kazumi Tokoroda, however, was different. She went to a prestigious private girls' school, and her grades were among the best in her class. Times had certainly changed.

Chikako Ishizu stepped forward and greeted the pair. "Thank you both for coming."

Harue, latching on to Chikako and Officer Fuchigami, looked pathetically happy to see them. "I'm so sorry we're late."

"Not at all. There's still five minutes." Chikako smiled cheerfully, and glanced at Kazumi. "Sorry you had to miss school today."

Kazumi hung back behind her mother a bit and, ignoring Chikako, spoke to Officer Fuchigami. "So where's the line-up going to be?"

"Follow me," came the crisp reply.

"Um, I—" Harue seemed rattled. "Are you sure it's all right if I'm not there with her?"

Before either of the policewomen could speak, Kazumi said impatiently, "It's *okay* already! How many times do they have to say it? I can't stand having you next to me, complaining about every little thing."

Chikako slid smoothly between the mother and daughter and took Harue by the arm. "Officer Fuchigami," she said, "will you escort Kazumi upstairs? I have some things I'd like her mother to take a look at over this way."

She guided the other woman out of the lobby, past the Traffic Division office, and into a small conference room. On a beat-up old table lay various articles that had been brought over from the Property Room. Clothing, shoes, a handkerchief, a memo book, folders—

Harue took one look, and flinched.

"These are your husband's personal effects, including the contents of his briefcase." Chikako pulled out a chair, offering it to the other woman. "To assist in the investigation, we also brought over quite a few items from your husband's desk and locker at work. We're ready to return them now, but we're not entirely sure which items were his, and which should be returned to the company. We thought you might be able to help."

"Oh . . . I see." She put a hand to her mouth, and nodded several times.

"To prevent any mistakes, we'd appreciate it very much if you'd take some time to look over the articles. Some of these will bring back memories of your husband, I'm sure, and the last thing we want to do is intrude on your privacy. Go ahead and take all the time you need. There's no hurry whatsoever." She indicated the interphone in the corner. "If anything comes up, just dial 221. You can always reach me at that number. If I'm tied up, I'll send Officer Fuchigami."

"All right."

"Can I get you a cold drink?"

"No, thank you. I'm fine." Harue's eyes filled with tears. "I'm sorry."

"Nothing to apologize for. Some of these things may have gotten a bit soiled in the process of examining them, although we did take every precaution. Also, you'll notice not all the articles of clothing he had on are here. Some we need to keep as evidence."

"Yes. Yes, I understand." Harue opened her small handbag, took out a handkerchief and dabbed her eyes. The handkerchief was faded from many washings. It dutifully absorbed her tears.

"Detective Ishizu." Hearing the note of pleading in her voice, Chikako sat down next to Harue.

"Yes?"

"My daughter—will Kazumi really be able to identify the killer? The police are going to bring out their real suspects now, aren't they? The people on TV say that friend of Miss Imai's is under suspicion, but that's not the whole story, is it? And that's why you need Kazumi's testimony. How many of them will there be? What happens to them if Kazumi can't identify any of them?"

Chikako smiled reassuringly. "It's true we're counting on your daughter's testimony, Mrs. Tokoroda, but even if nothing comes of today's attempt, the investigation won't stall, I promise. Don't worry."

"She won't be coming face to face with them, will she? They won't have any reason to hold this against her?"

"Not at all. They won't even be able to see her. We'll keep her out of harm's way."

Harue crumpled her handkerchief. "It hasn't been in the papers that Kazumi saw the killer. I haven't seen it on the news, or anywhere."

"That's right. We haven't given out that information. She's in no danger." Chikako patted Harue lightly on the arm. "Besides, there's no guarantee that whoever she saw was the actual killer. It's just that we want to know all we can about everyone who was in any way involved with your husband before he died—no matter how seemingly tenuous the connection. That's why we've asked Kazumi for her help."

Harue stared at the pile of belongings on the table and said in a low voice, "She's very angry."

"She is?"

"Oh, yes. She's furious that her father was murdered. Very, very angry with the killer." Shaking her head, she added swiftly, "Of course, I despise whoever took my husband's life. But I'm still just so shattered by it all . . . somehow I can't get used to the fact that he's gone, it's just so . . . shocking. My mind is reeling, trying to take it in. I'm not a strong person, I guess, but I just can't seem to work up any anger."

"Your feelings are perfectly natural," Chikako told her gently. "I think if I were in your situation, that's exactly how I'd feel."

"A policewoman like you?"

"We're just like anybody else. You aren't a weak person by any means."

A teardrop trickled out of Harue's eye and fell, landing on the back of her hand.

"Kazumi is strong."

"Yes, she seems very grown-up."

"You know, she's got much more strength of mind than I do. Her father was like that. She gets it from him. I know why she lashes out at me—it's because it irritates her to see me crying and dithering all the time, acting like such a fool."

Harue probably had no one else she could talk to like this. Chikako decided to stay and listen.

"She swears she'll find the killer herself and make him pay. Or her."

"Really?"

"'I swear I'll get revenge. I'll kill whoever did it.' She says that too."

"She's said that to you?"

"Not to me, not in so many words. But I heard her on the phone with a friend—her boyfriend actually—and she was getting pretty excited, and saying those things. It was her cell phone. You know, you can call from anywhere with those . . . I just happened to overhear."

"When was this?"

"A few days ago. At home."

"Who's her boyfriend again?" Chikako instantly recalled his name and face, but she pretended to be struggling to remember.

"His name's Tatsuya Ishiguro—she met him through one of her classmates. A nice boy. Well, not a boy, really—he's older than she is, about twenty, I think."

"I never heard directly from Kazumi about him, but I think Officer Fuchigami did. I get the idea it's a pretty serious relationship, though, right?" Laughing, Chikako said, "Totally mad about each other?"

Harue gave a little laugh. The rims of her eyes were red. "I've only met him once or twice. He's never actually been over to the house. I've caught glimpses of him when he's come to pick her up."

Chikako nodded.

"Kazumi tells him everything, you know. She's never said a word to me about what happened to her father, but she does seem to talk about it with that boy. Why, she was on the phone with him this morning right up until we went out the door. She got herself all worked up. She's just determined to catch the killer herself."

Chikako said quietly, "We need to be careful not to overexcite her. That would only make things more difficult for her."

Harue went on in a monotone, "She doesn't turn to me for support at all. But I can understand. It's because I'm not strong, the way she is."

She sounded intensely lonely. She fell silent, and for a while Chikako shared the silence with her. As the quiet in the room bore down on Harue, Chikako stayed by her side and offered a hand, helping to support the weight of the silence.

That was really all she could do for this woman who was hurt, and frightened, and grieving. She found it deeply frustrating, maddening even, to be able to do no more. But long experience as a police officer had taught Chikako one thing: the determination to do all you could to help people and be of service, although indispensable, was not enough. No less necessary—still more necessary, in fact—was the patience to bear with yourself through all the times when you could not help a soul, when you were of no damn use to anybody.

After a pause, Harue apologized yet again. "Please forgive me for going on like that."

Chikako stood up. "Are you all right now?"

"Yes. Sorry."

"If it's too painful for you to look these things over today, you can always do it another time, you know."

"Thank you, but I'll be fine now." She wiped her eyes, lightly pressed the end of her nose with the handkerchief, and sat up straight in her chair. Then she reached a hand toward the pile of her dead husband's effects.

"I'll bring Kazumi here as soon as she's finished, so don't worry." With this, Chikako left the room and went back into the corridor. She poked her head into the Traffic Division office and instructed one of the girls there to take Harue a cup of coffee in half an hour. Then she started back upstairs.

The Tokorodas had met at work, she recalled. They must have made an attractive couple. As a young woman, Harue must have been the sweet, quiet type that men instinctively want to protect. Was that what had attracted Ryosuke Tokoroda to her? What had he truly thought of his wife? He had been fond of looking after young girls and having them lean on him; perhaps such activities had absorbed him to the point where his wife, now rather the worse for wear, no longer occupied his thoughts. He had been about to let his old house go and purchase a new one; if it were equally easy to trade in an old wife for a new one, would he have done so?

The thought was dispiriting. Chikako squared her shoulders, trying to snap back into character.

Chikako Ishizu had not initially been involved in the Ryosuke Tokoroda homicide case. She was not in that echelon in Suginami precinct. Being transferred back from the Metropolitan Police Department to a precinct was not all that unusual; it could happen for a variety of reasons. In Chikako's case, however, it had clearly been a demotion. She had not gone straight to Suginami, having first put in a year or so in the Criminal Affairs Division at Marunouchi precinct, mostly filing papers. Then she was transferred to the Suginami precinct, officially in the Criminal Affairs Division but in reality serving as an irregular. Again, most of her time was spent sorting and filing papers, and serving as liaison on continuing investigations.

The case she had worked on four years earlier as part of the MPD arson squad had been bizarre in the extreme, and cost a great many lives. Under the circumstances, Chikako had taken it on herself to do all she humanly could to solve the case, but that had meant flouting regulations and, as a result, getting kicked downstairs.

And yet she was by no means as irate or resentful about her treatment as many around her assumed. Having come up directly against a criminal case and a set of phenomena that were, quite simply, extraordinary, she had been forced into the realization that those events were out of whack with everyday society. That type of case just could not be contained within the sturdy framework of traditional understanding that, for good or for ill, held sway in the police force. All this had come to seem to her quite unavoidable, indeed entirely natural. Also, in order to distance herself awhile in time and space from the darker aspect of the police organization of which that earlier experience had afforded her a glimpse, and to work out her own way of not yielding to it, nothing could have suited Chikako better than to be detached temporarily from the MPD.

Still, with her history, Chikako was something of a black sheep at the Suginami Police Station, a hanger-on with no chance of being accepted as "one of the boys." All the more reason why, three days into the homicide investigation there, she had been astonished to receive an abrupt summons and be handed orders to help guard the Tokoroda home. Compared with that moment, the sudden order a few days back to join this unusual plan had elicited barely a ripple of surprise in her.

They needed a woman's help, her superior had explained, sounding (Chikako thought) like a neighborhood council member asking a local housewife to assist at somebody's funeral. There was no use taking offense at every little thing, though, and so she heard him out. It turned out that Mrs. Tokoroda and her daughter, distracted and nervous after losing the mainstay of the family, required immediate police protection. The task was not distasteful to her. She quickly accepted the assignment and was introduced to Officer Fuchigami, with whom she would be teamed.

Barely three days after Ryosuke Tokoroda's murder, the personal link between him and Naoko Imai, the earlier homicide victim in Shibuya, had already come to light. The investigating teams were abuzz with the possibility of a serial killer on the loose. However, the decision to provide extra protection for the Tokoroda home did not arise organically out of the police investigation, but was prompted by a direct request from Kazumi.

For several months now, the teenager said, she had been harassed by prank phone calls; moreover, she had been followed on her way home from school. The voice on the phone belonged to a young man, and whoever was tailing her appeared to be, as far as she could tell, no more than twenty years old. Possibly they were the same individual.

"I told Dad what was happening and he was really worried, so some mornings he used to walk me to the train station. No one ever followed us, but then I got a phone call warning me that if I thought having my dad tag along with me meant I'd be safe, I could think again."

The message had given her the creeps, but nothing happened for a couple of weeks and she'd started to forget about it—until this awful thing happened to her dad, and then she got to worrying again, she said.

She had no idea who her stalker might be. "I get along great with my boyfriend, and the guys I dated or hung out with in groups before that never made any kind of trouble. So I figure it must be strictly one-way. Somebody I don't even know, living in his own little fantasy world. But then I started thinking—what if it's got something to do with my dad's murder, what do I do?"

The investigators were fairly convinced that the homicide of Ryosuke Tokoroda had not been an isolated event, and so the premise did not sit well with them that someone stalking Kazumi had deliberately murdered her father, knowing that she had gone to him for aid and that he had taken steps to protect her. Still, stranger things had happened. Besides, in the days immediately after a murder, any lead was worth following. So they put a police guard on the Tokoroda widow and daughter, and kept the house under surveillance. That was where the need for "a woman's help" came in.

The first time she ever met Kazumi, Chikako had thought she seemed extremely scared. At that point the girl's fear had outweighed her anger, dominating her emotional landscape entirely.

The age gap came into play, Chikako quickly getting to know Harue Tokoroda while Kazumi warmed to Officer Fuchigami. Although assigned to protect the pair from danger, they were not put on strict alert as when guarding a witness, and the atmosphere was quite relaxed. Officer Fuchigami came and went in plainclothes, accompanying Kazumi on shopping expeditions and the like, and when she stayed overnight at Kazumi's request, she slept on an extra futon in her bedroom like a girlfriend over for a slumber party.

When the two homicide investigations merged, Chikako and Officer Fuchigami were still guarding the Tokoroda home. It was about a week later that the decision was made to alter security arrangements, downgrading them to regular patrols by the local police box.

That decision was not made unilaterally by the homicide investigation team, of course; the Tokorodas themselves had indicated that special protection was no longer necessary. As far as Captain Shimojima, head of the investigation, was concerned, since neither Chikako nor Fuchigami had been part of the original team they could easily be spared for the assignment, and for safety's sake he would have preferred that they kept an eye on things a bit longer. But Kazumi Tokoroda, now looking very downcast, had begun to back down from her previous statements about the stalker. Certainly during the two policewomen's watch there hadn't been a single harassing phone call, and no suspicious characters had been seen hanging around the house. All had remained quiet.

It was certainly conceivable that the stalker was biding his time, scared off by the heightened security. But the investigators' attention was focused by now on Miss A, and no one regarded the stalker as a serious lead anymore. Suppose the crime *had* been committed by a man targeting Kazumi: until then he had lain so low that even Kazumi had "started to forget about" him by her own admission, so why would he swing into action not by approaching her directly, but by leapfrogging over her to carry out a lethal attack on her father? It made no sense. The case against Miss A was far more compelling.

Harue Tokoroda did not mean to second-guess her daughter on the need for police protection, but the thought of the two of them being left suddenly on their own made her a bit nervous; would it be all right if she turned to

Chikako now and then for advice? Naturally, Chikako urged her not to hesitate to get in touch. She phoned daily thereafter and dropped by the house every few days or so, always taking care to spend at least some time with Harue. Her exclusion from the investigation proper made such attentions possible. Staying on in the house longer wouldn't be a bad idea, either, she thought. The sad part was, even though such contact was every bit as necessary as the investigation per se, the need for it went virtually unrecognized within the police structure.

"I'm not worried about the stalker anymore. I'm sorry I ever brought it up." After so declaring, Kazumi had in fact stopped acting frightened. Instead, her anger was surfacing ever more visibly. The switch in feelings probably reflected her assumption that Miss A was the killer, thought Chikako. Tokoroda's involvement in an illicit relationship with a young woman roughly the age of his daughter had perhaps led to his murder: for Kazumi, that supposition must have been hard to swallow. Even so, she had apparently decided to wait patiently until Miss A was arrested.

But then, before long Kazumi came out with brand-new testimony. The gist of it was that several times over the course of the last six months, happening to see her father around town, she'd noticed he was in the company of people unknown to her.

"There was the Sunday I saw him at the train station, standing with someone else on the opposite platform, and the time I saw him sitting in his car in the parking lot of the supermarket where my mom usually shops, talking to someone through the car window on the driver's side. Also, twice someone called the house asking for him, and when I said he was out, they just hung up. One time (I forget if it was after the first call or the second), I hung up the phone and then happened to look out the window and see someone loitering by the hedge. That was the third stranger. Of course, I didn't think much of it at the time. I figured maybe someone was asking directions, or he'd run into an old friend, or whatever. The phone business was weird, but nothing really happened after that so I let it go. I don't think I ever told my mom or my dad."

While detectives were taking down this new testimony, they were also combing the hard drive of Ryosuke Tokoroda's laptop computer. As a result of that search, it became clear that in addition to his friends and acquaintances at work and at home, Tokoroda had been associating with a circle of Internet friends as well.

The laptop had preserved an eloquent record of all Tokoroda's doings in cyberspace. His harmless surfing and exchanges with email friends, including colleagues from work, were typical and unremarkable. He had apparently not corresponded with Naoko Imai, whose name did not crop up here. (According to her friends she was uninterested in computers, preferring to send messages by cell phone.)

The investigation team had anticipated that Ryosuke Tokoroda probably haunted dating sites, seeking out young girls to approach, but contrary to expectation they turned up no trace of any such activity. What they did find was something utterly beyond all expectation.

Ryosuke Tokoroda had created an alternate "family" on the Internet.

There was a wife and daughter and son; a shadow family of four in all. They had called one another "Dad," "Mom," "Kazumi," and "Minoru," sending frequent emails back and forth, and chatting online as well. Nor had their acquaintance been limited to the Internet; the foursome had met up face-to-face at least once. And Tokoroda had sent "Kazumi" an email indicating he wanted to see her again.

The police checked immediately with Harue Tokoroda, but the screen name "Mom" did not belong to her, nor was "Kazumi" the real Kazumi Tokoroda. On this point, mother and daughter were in complete agreement: they never suspected that Ryosuke Tokoroda was involved in any such charade. Harue knew next to nothing about the Internet anyway, and seemed at first to have difficulty making sense of what the detectives were trying to tell her.

"I guess he wasn't satisfied with us," said Kazumi. "Not that we were with him, either." She went on savagely, "*Playing house* with total strangers? Are you kidding me? He was running away from us, that's what. God! Who the hell knows what he could have been thinking!"

Her anger was understandable. Chikako regretted from the bottom of her heart that Ryosuke Tokoroda had died. He should have lived, and faced the brunt of Kazumi's wrath. In any case, it was rare for a man's death to lay open his deepest secrets, one after another, this blatantly.

"Now you've *got* to catch whoever killed him. Is it that Miss A, or who-ever? The one they're all talking about? If it is, you let me talk to her."

Chikako soothed her, saying they still didn't know.

Kazumi's eyes then flashed a challenge, and her fists clenched as she spoke. "Well, as soon as you find out for sure who did it, let me in, okay? I want to ask one little question. I want to know, 'Why did you kill my dad? What was it about him that made you want to kill him? What did he ever do?' I have a right to know that, don't I? Ever since he died, we've been find-ing out all these horrible things that we'd never have known otherwise. It's humiliating, and it hurts, and . . . it stinks."

A thoroughly understandable plea. A legitimate complaint. Chikako longed to tell the girl what it was she wanted to know.

But to do that, first they had to catch the killer.

Chikako was well aware that the joint investigation team was frantically going after Miss A, determined to bring her to bay. Were they not even the slightest bit uneasy with that conclusion? Was it the right approach? The true motive and killer might well lie hidden elsewhere, she thought—within Ryosuke Tokoroda's secret life. Was it not wrong-headed to let that go unex-plored?

The unknown multiple figures whom Kazumi reported having seen together with Ryosuke Tokoroda—why not investigate them? Why focus exclusively on Miss A?

As she was fretting over these questions, the summons had come to par-ticipate in today's session. And then she had learned that a group of detec-tives on the joint investigation team—albeit a minority—shared her doubts. As she listened to them, however, she realized that their speculations far exceeded and transcended her own. Her heart ached for Harue and Kazumi.

And that was why she was here today.

That the desk sergeant was her old friend Etsuro Takegami had come as a surprise, but not that he'd been the one to step up as Sergeant Nakamoto's replacement. That was the kind of man Takegami was and always had been.

Detective Akizu seemed to be under some misapprehension about their past; she and Takegami had never had an intimate personal relationship, and any idea that he'd worshipped her from afar was just plain silly. She was three years older than him, and when they first met, both had been married. There had never been even a glimmer of romance. It was just that they had worked well together, had felt an immediate bond. Since then they had taken quite different paths, but it pleased her to see that Takegami remained his old self. She hoped that in the eyes of that rough, honest cop, she herself did not appear too awfully changed.

A thought struck her. To *appear* a certain way, and to *be* a certain way—which was real? What to Ryosuke Tokoroda had been true, and what false? Would his daughter's anger have been comprehensible to him?

Yes, Kazumi was in a continual state of rage, just as her mother had said. From the first moment she'd spotted her in the lobby earlier, deep down Chikako had been taken aback at the level of anger clearly distinguishable on the girl's face. Her unconcealed anger was half due to her youth. What accounted for the other half? Perhaps the events of this afternoon would lay that bare.

6

This was Takegami's first meeting with Kazumi Tokoroda. He had filed many a statement from her, and studied them all carefully, but never before had he looked her in the face—gazed straight into her eyes.

He knew she was an A student, and she definitely gave the impression of being a young lady with a quick mind, he thought. She seemed rather nervous; her greeting was stiff and curt. Takegami for his part was in no mood to play the part of a benign, avuncular figure. What this intelligent girl wanted from him now was not kindness and compassion, he could tell, but a brisk and businesslike approach. He acted accordingly.

"I'm going to summon three people to this room, and question each one in turn."

She nodded silently.

"All three carried on an email correspondence with your father. I won't go into their names and ages, what sort of people they are, or what the nature of their association with your father may have been; that should all come out naturally in the course of the questioning."

Then Takegami's face softened a bit. "I'm sure you've already been told this, but let me emphasize again that we've brought you here not so much to hear what these people have to say, as to pick up on how they say it. Their voices, mannerisms, gestures—that sort of thing. So don't let yourself be overly distracted by either the questions I ask or the answers they may give. Is that clear?"

Kazumi nodded, again without speaking. Takegami became curious: when she did answer, was she the type who said "Okay," "Yes, sir," or what?

"You're tense, aren't you? Everything all right?"

Kazumi looked down, and made a fanning gesture at her face. "It's awfully hot in here."

"I'll have them switch on the air conditioning." Tokunaga got up and went out into the corridor.

Once the door had closed behind him, Kazumi fixed her eyes on it and said in a stiff and emotionless tone: "Look, don't just tell me these are people who 'carried on an email correspondence' with my dad, all right? Give it to me straight. The ones coming in here are 'Mom' and 'Minoru' and 'Kazumi,' aren't they?" As she finished speaking, she looked straight at Takegami.

"That's right," he answered. "I didn't want you forming any preconceptions, that's all."

"I'm not stupid, you know." She threw the words out sharply, then motioned with a tilt of her head as she asked, "So, I'll be in a room over there?"

"Yes, on the other side of that two-way mirror. They won't be able to see you from here." He went and stood in front of the mirror. "You don't have to worry about that."

Kazumi went over to the mirror and touched it with a fingertip. "I watch police dramas on TV. I know you use rooms like this for line-ups."

"Not always, actually. In fact, today we'll be doing something a little different."

"You stand them in a row against the wall, right?" She turned around abruptly. "And tell them one by one to step forward or turn to the right or whatever. Isn't that what you do in here?"

"We thought that in this case, that approach might be all the more confusing for you."

"Huh." She looked contemptuous, as if she wanted to say it again. *I'm not stupid.*

"And there is something else. Bear with me for repeating instructions you've no doubt already been told. Even if you do recognize one of the three people, and make a clear identification, that in itself does not automatically make that person a suspect in your father's killing. So you can go ahead and relax."

"I *am* relaxed."

Takegami gave a slight smile.

Kazumi put her face up close to the two-way mirror, her nose almost touching it. "What do you know—you really can't see through it, can you? It's no different from a regular mirror."

"Yes, like I said."

"But ten to one the people coming here today have seen police dramas on TV and in the movies, just like me, so don't you think they'll put two and two together? Realize I'm watching them from the other side, I mean."

"They may have an idea that they're being watched, but they certainly won't know it's you."

Kazumi then said, not to Takegami but to Officer Fuchigami standing over by the door, "You know what? Since yesterday I've been trying all kinds of ways to sharpen my recollections."

After a quick glance Takegami's way, the young policewoman replied, "Is that right? How have you been getting on?"

Kazumi knitted her trim eyebrows into a frown, looking glum. "I think I made it worse. The more I try to pin them down, the more they slip away."

"That's bound to happen," Officer Fuchigami said soothingly. "I'm sure the best thing is to just be natural."

"If you don't want to go through with this, we can end it right here," said Takegami.

Kazumi's reaction was swift. "No. No, I'll do it." She shook her head emphatically, her chestnut hair swinging silkily. "I'm okay with it, really I am. I can do it."

"I appreciate that. Still, don't push yourself. If you've had enough, all you have to do is say so, any time you want."

"I'll be fine. But there is one thing." Her gaze intensified. "What if I wanted you to ask them a certain question or, you know, have someone make a certain gesture or something? What would I do then?"

Takegami cocked his head a little, displaying his right ear. "See something that looks like a hearing aid? That's an earphone. It's connected to the room next door. If anything like that occurs to you, just tell Detective Ishizu or Officer Fuchigami. You'll also be able to hear everything said in this room, through a highly directional microphone."

Kazumi smiled, as if her mind were finally at ease. She asked to go to the bathroom before they got started, and went out with Officer Fuchigami.

As they left the room, Tokunaga came back in. He raised his heavy eyebrows a bit and asked, "How old is she again?"

"Sixteen."

"Going on twenty, I'd say. Her makeup job is perfect. Doesn't go with her way of talking, though, which strikes me as a bit rough."

"What do you expect? You'll never make the grade these days if you let a thing like that bother you."

"Make the grade as what? A cop, or as somebody's date?" Tokunaga said drily, turning up one corner of his mouth.

"That's right, you're still a batch, aren't you."

"A *batch*? As in bachelor? Please! Nobody says that nowadays."

"I'm surrounded by men who can't get a wife. They're piling up three-deep."

"We're all after your daughter. Noriko, isn't it? I hear she's a looker."

"Where'd you hear that?"

"Dumb-Ass, mostly."

Takegami snorted and sat down. "Who, Akizu? I don't know who might be after her, but I doubt him. He's famous for getting into scrapes with one woman after another. Calls it his 'dame troubles.'"

"Somehow that doesn't surprise me."

Takegami pictured his daughter's face. *If my Noriko were to wear a look like the one on Kazumi Tokoroda's face just now, what would it mean? If she were to step into an interrogation room or be seated behind a two-way mirror, how would she react?* "I brought her up the best I could," he murmured. "And now she's going out with a cop."

Tokunaga whistled.

"She had a boyfriend at college, but she dumped him for this guy. Happened just the other day."

"Sounds like a young lady with a compassionate heart. If only there were more like her. Love your local underpaid public servant."

"I don't know if it's compassion, but I gotta say, her old boyfriend was better looking than the new guy, even if he is a cop."

"Looks don't matter for men. Or for women." Tokunaga recited, "'Though in the evening he may boast of rosy cheeks, yet in the morning he lies dead, a heap of bones—.' Here 'rosy cheeks' means good looks."

"Ryosuke Tokoroda was good-looking."

"And unfaithful to his better half. Not that everybody who's attractive is a cheat. But the two together is certainly a recipe for unhappiness."

Takegami laughed. "'Better half'? Now *there's* an old-fashioned expression!"

After the affair with Naoko Imai surfaced, the investigators had no choice but to examine all the particulars of Ryosuke Tokoroda's dealings with women; the upshot was that Harue Tokoroda, already in shock from her husband's death, faced a barrage of new and painful questions. Whether the detective who interrogated her was a seasoned veteran, or whether the woman's own personality had determined the result, Takegami could not tell; but the finished report was a marvel of thoroughness, with an attachment giving Harue's contribution verbatim. Not having been present at the interview, Takegami had no way of knowing what expression she may have worn while being questioned on such things. But as he read her statement, her apparent lack of any psychological resistance filled him with sympathy, while at the same time giving him a sense of something unfathomable and elusive.

"Yes," she had replied, "my husband definitely had a wandering eye. In all our twenty years of marriage, I'd say there was never a year when he wasn't mixed up in some sort of trouble over another woman. He liked them young. Probably all men do, as far as that goes, but in my husband's case he was also good at being liked by them. It's a funny thing for a wife to say, but he did have a knack for making girlfriends. In the beginning, of course, it used to drive me crazy. Once when Kazumi was still a baby I decided that I'd had enough, and took her home with me to my parents. Well, that crushed him. He came to get me, as contrite as could be, saying it was all his fault. But when that wore off he was right back at his old tricks again. It happened over and over.

"If we hadn't had Kazumi right away, I might not have been able to stand it. But you know . . . once, after we'd been married about ten years, I got to thinking. Why does a man who runs around with other women always come home to me, night after night after night? He never once deserted Kazumi and me, or neglected us. Anyone who didn't know better would have thought he was the most devoted husband and father in the world, I'm sure. Because he was so good to us.

"So I came to the conclusion that his playing around must be a kind of sickness. The other thing was, even though he had a lot of girlfriends he wasn't intimate with them all; around most of them he acted like a big brother, funny as that may sound. I think it came down to one thing: he loved fussing over girls and having them fuss over him. That's all there was to it. If a girl wanted something from him, he couldn't say no.

"He had a pretty good-paying job at Orion Foods, but nothing special; we were never wealthy. But I will say this: he never threw money around on his girlfriends at Kazumi's and my expense. I suppose he had to do some fancy finagling to be able to show them a good time. I wasn't happy about Kazumi's being an only child, but he said children cost money and one was enough, so I gave up on having any more. From his viewpoint, of course, one more mouth to feed would have meant that much less pocket money.

"Oh, how he doted on Kazumi! He was thrilled when she was born. He said he'd always wanted a daughter, that he'd always dreamed of being the father of a little girl. Not long ago he had to write something for the in-house magazine at work, and he wrote about how much he was looking forward to walking his daughter down the aisle on her wedding day.

"So no, no matter how many times he was unfaithful to me, I don't think he ever meant to break up his family. It's possible he thought there'd be no harm done as long as I never found out. That's ridiculous—of *course* I was going to find out—but in that respect he was a happy-go-lucky sort of guy. He had no idea I thought that about him, I'm sure.

"About Naoko Imai, I can't tell you anything. I suppose she was another of his girlfriends. How close they may have been I have no way of knowing, but the idea that the relationship might have been intimate at first and then evolved into more of a friendship, or a brother–sister sort of thing, doesn't surprise me. As I said, my husband liked that type of arrangement.

"Divorce? Never. He never once said the word to me. At one point I thought about it in private, but that was a good ten years ago . . . You see, when I reached the conclusion that his misbehavior was a kind of disease, I decided that leaving him wasn't the answer, that I'd only be worse off that way.

"Suppose I had gotten tough. Suppose I'd asked him if he had any idea how much pain he was causing me with every betrayal. He would have been at a complete loss. I take care of my family, he'd have said. And he'd have been right.

"I may be too good-natured, but somehow I couldn't hate him. I could never stay mad. He was like a child—a little boy. I'll be like a mother to him, or an older sister, I thought, and if we get along, what's wrong with that? As we both got older, we'd have had no choice but to lean on each other anyway.

"What did Kazumi think about it all? Well, she's a normal teenager, and she did get wind of her father's habits. But at her age I really think if it wasn't that it would be something else. Teenage girls can be awfully hard on their fathers, rebellious, you know? At home, the two of them were barely on speaking terms over the past year or two. My husband wanted to get through to her, and he tried, but she just wasn't having any of it. I did feel a little sorry for him, but he only brought it on himself. Actually, I suppose I was hoping she could get him to take a good, hard look at himself.

"Well, yes . . . in that sense, his affair with Naoko Imai *is* especially hard to take. Just the idea that he would seek out someone that young to have an affair with, when his own daughter was old enough to be dating. I suppose he never saw any connection between the two.

"Kazumi is partly angry with me, too. For being under his thumb, for letting him do as he pleased. She used to scold me sometimes for not establishing my own identity. 'Mom, what kind of life do you have?' she'd say. I would tell her that how I lived my life was *my* business, and that there were things between a husband and wife that she couldn't hope to understand at her age. I hoped she had the brains to understand what I meant—or anyway to think it over, and try to understand.

"I'm sure that as a mother, Kazumi thinks of me as a cowardly good-for-nothing. Especially the way I am now with him gone, so lost and so sad . . . I can guess it aggravates her no end."

Reading this long soliloquy of Harue's in the report, Nakamoto had been filled with amazement. Some wives were certainly forbearing. "I suppose there are couples like this out there. The marriage probably works for them. Their kids are a different story, though."

Takegami had replied that personally, he didn't trust anybody who referred to herself as "too good-natured."

Nakamoto had roared with laughter. "You've got a point there, Gami. Good one."

Going over the same territory with Kazumi Tokoroda must have required even greater tact. This report was short.

"You've probably heard all this already from my mom," it began. "Anyway, I knew my dad was hanging out with young girls. I mean, it was *sooo* obvious. But I didn't know anything about Naoko Imai. She was really recent, wasn't she?

"Ask my mom, she'll tell you the same thing—ever since I was in junior high, my dad's been hypercritical of me. He and I were always squaring off. Lately I avoided talking to him, period. The minute I opened my mouth he'd come down on me, hard. For staying out late, talking too much on my cell phone—he never had *anything* good to say about my boyfriend Tatsuya—or for being a smart-aleck, not appreciating all he did for me, that kind of thing. Tatsuya said the thought of me growing up and going off to live my own life made Dad lonely, and after that I kind of felt sorry for him and thought maybe I ought to treat him nicer, but when we were in the same room it never worked out.

"Maybe once I got a little older and was out on my own I could soften up towards him, I thought, but not now. And instead of always going at it tooth and nail, I figured it was better just to chill out and not let him get to me, so for the past year I made a point of totally ignoring him. That wasn't the only reason. I knew he was busy at work, under a lot of stress, so why stir up trouble when he was home?"

Harue Tokoroda had confirmed this; father and daughter had been waging a cold war.

At the time of this report, Kazumi had still been cowering in fear of the alleged stalker, and she had been assigned a bodyguard. The detective who filed the report had appended an opinion to the effect that under the circumstances, Kazumi Tokoroda's range of thinking was severely affected, and once the matter of the stalker had been cleared up it might be a good idea to take down her story again. Takegami had thought at the time that this showed good insight. He still thought so.

Eventually the stalker lead had dried up, and at approximately the same time, the existence of Ryosuke Tokoroda's shadow family in cyberspace came to light. Harue and Kazumi had then been revisited for questioning. Harue was of the opinion that her husband's involvement with this other "family" was a form of socializing similar to his philandering.

"I heard from people in his section at work that the young women employees used to call him 'Papa' or 'Big Brother.' Now I'm sure that was meant in a joking way, but even so, if he hadn't liked it, they would hardly have told me about it, would they? My husband got along beautifully with the people who worked for him. Not just the women, the men, too. So many of them came to the funeral. He cared about them, and he looked after them. Maybe that's what made him 'Papa' in their eyes. Those people he was communicating with on the Internet were young. I suppose that's why he picked a nickname like that."

Harue doubted that the association had amounted to a substitute family.

Kazumi took a different view. She was furious. Perhaps her father's unfaithfulness might be written off, but not this. The idea that he had been playing "family" with a bunch of strangers was, to her, unforgivable.

"I don't know what to think. But I'll tell you, it really pisses me off. He may have had things against my mom and me, but we had them against him too. Didn't he ever stop to think how it would make us *feel* for him to do a thing like that right under our noses? What makes it worse is that one of them had the same name as me. So what if it's only a screen name, not her real name—like that makes any difference! You've got to find those people. I want to know what made them kill my dad. And I want to know what the hell he was writing to them."

After this angry outburst, Kazumi began letting on that she had seen her father around town in the company of strangers. Until then, she had never mentioned any such thing.

Nakamoto had suggested at the time that Kazumi's anger was making it impossible for her to distinguish between what she imagined and what she had actually seen and heard. "She says she can never forgive the killer, but it sounds to me like it's her old man she can never forgive. In any case, her story's been changing every five minutes. Any new statement from her should be taken with two grains of salt."

Takegami had felt the same way. Way back then, that's what the two of them had said. And Nakamoto had only grown more and more convinced. "You know, Gami," he'd said, "I'm just not buying that other theory. No way is Miss A the perp."

Takegami's reflections were interrupted by the sound of Chikako Ishizu's voice in his ear: "We're ready. Kazumi's in her seat. Any time you're ready."

Takegami glanced at the two-way mirror. No sign of the women's faces there, of course. All he saw reflected was his own face, set to enter the batter's box.

Catching sight of Takegami's face, Tokunaga nodded in confirmation. He picked up the interphone receiver. "All right, tell them to send in the first one."

From: Mom
To: Kazumi
Subject: Urgent

Have you heard what's happened to Dad? I must see you
right away.

From: Mom
To: Minoru
Subject: Urgent

```
Something terrible has happened to Dad. Let's meet right
away.
```

From: Kazumi
To: Mom
Subject: Tell me

Did *you* kill him?

1

A thin young man came into the room. His shoulders appeared bony through the raggedy white T-shirt he was wearing. His jeans, too, were well worn; only his blue-and-yellow sneakers looked brand-new, their rubber soles squeaking on the floor as he walked in.

Takegami stood up to greet him, motioning for him to sit in the chair opposite. The youth kept his eyes on the uniformed officer who ushered him in, watching until he went out and closed the door. Even then he made no move to turn and look at Takegami.

"Have a seat," said Takegami. He was dismayed to realize that he was extremely nervous.

Making no move to sit down, the young man swung his head toward Takegami and gave him a silent once-over. Next he looked at Tokunaga, and then he let his gaze roam from the table in the center of the room to the window, the wall mirror, and the wall phone before darting another look at the door.

If each spot his gaze landed on was represented by a dot, and if those dots were connected by lines, probably the resulting figure would represent a constellation of some significance. Probably a cop with experience in interrogation would be able to rattle off its name. But Takegami's stargazing days were long gone. He had forgotten the names of all the stars he'd ever known.

"Go ahead and sit down, it's okay." The words were informal. Probably they came out that way because he was trying to make himself relax, but once out of his mouth he was afraid they would have the opposite effect. This would never do.

Finally the youth turned to face Takegami, and asked in a surprisingly resonant tone, "Is this where you interrogate people?"

Takegami gave him a smile. "That's right. But as I think has already been explained to you, you are not under investigation. We have some questions we hope you can help us out with, and because they concern a rather delicate matter, we wanted to handle it sub rosa. So this was the best place to meet."

"Sub rosa?" The youth repeated the words uncomprehendingly, cocking his head.

"Confidentially. So other people won't hear."

"Got it."

After this terse reply, the youth seated himself. He sat erect, spine against the chair back, and folded his hands by his waist, then pressed them tightly against himself.

Takegami introduced himself and had Tokunaga do the same. The youth returned each of their greetings with a thrust of his chin. He moved jerkily. *The kid's nervous too*, thought Takegami, *and why not?*

"Let's start with your name and address." Takegami ran his finger along one of the forms in front of him, tracing Nakamoto's neat writing. "You're Minoru Kitajo, is that correct? And you live in Hachioji, at—."

Minoru Kitajo confirmed that the name and street address were both his. His voice was oddly strained. Seated across from him, Takegami could see the tension in his crossed arms.

"Born in 1983. That makes you what, eighteen?"

"My birthday's in November, so I'm still seventeen."

"Okay. Says here you're unemployed. What about school?"

"I quit. Last year."

"Dropped out, eh? And you're living with your parents?"

"More or less. I'm renting an apartment near them, or I guess they're renting it for me."

"They pay the rent?"

"Yes."

"You work part-time anywhere?"

"Off and on I do. When I got my computer my dad only paid half, so I earned the rest working in a convenience store." Minoru said all this in one breath, then abruptly looked up. "Hey, Officer, aren't you forgetting something?"

Takegami felt a jolt of surprise. "What do you mean?" Tokunaga was sitting with his back half turned toward them, but in the mirror Takegami could make out the look of puzzlement on his face, brows raised in a query.

"You know—isn't there something you're supposed to say?" Minoru smirked. "'You have the right to remain silent, anything you do or say may be used against you in court,' and the whole bit. Like on TV."

Takegami laughed. A genuine laugh, not a play-acting one.

"You're not a suspect, so there's no need to warn you," he said. "You're not under arrest."

"Huh. So that's it."

"But no lying, all right? You'd only confuse the situation, and anyway in most cases it doesn't take much digging for us to find out when someone's been less than truthful. You wouldn't be doing yourself any favors. So I want you to answer all my questions honestly, without hiding any information, all right?"

"'In most cases'?" Minoru slumped down in the chair and looked up at the gray ceiling. "So you're saying that sometimes you *don't* find out."

"That's true. But that still doesn't make it okay to lie."

"As long as nobody finds out, what's the difference?"

"So you're saying it's ethically and morally okay to lie?"

Minoru suddenly relaxed and put his elbows up on the table. He looked Takegami straight in the face. "Officer, you're a funny guy."

"I'll take that as a compliment."

Kazumi Tokoroda was beautiful even in profile. Sitting on her left, a chair between them, Chikako had a clear view of the graceful lines of the girl's chin and throat.

As soon as the interrogation-room door opened, Kazumi had leaned forward until her forehead was practically touching the two-way mirror. She stared intently without blinking. Only when Takegami laughed and Minoru Kitajo crossed his arms and started talking did she sit back up. Then she reached inside the small cloth bag on her lap, fished around, and pulled out her cell phone.

Chikako gave her a quizzical look. Sensing the policewoman's eyes, Kazumi asked, still holding the cell phone, "Can I use my phone? A call just came in. It's an email. I need to send an answer."

"Go right ahead, as long as you don't make any noise. But won't that distract you?"

"Not as much as leaving it unanswered would."

The girl did seem fidgety.

"All right, go ahead."

Immediately, Kazumi began composing a message with deft moves of her right thumb. She apparently knew the locations of the letters by heart: her eyes remained fixed on the two-way mirror as she manipulated the buttons with amazing speed, never faltering or stopping to feel her way. Chikako had often observed people doing this on the train and elsewhere, but at such close range the feat was even more impressive.

The only time Kazumi looked down at the phone in her hand was after finishing her message, to push the "send" button.

"Who'd you write back to?" Chikako had intended the question to sound cheerfully innocuous, but Kazumi instantly stiffened.

"A friend."

Her tone was curt.

"I think I know why you want to talk to me," Minoru Kitajo said with a shrug of his knobby shoulders. "It's got something to do with the Tokoroda murder case, right? But you already know who did it. I saw it on the news."

"You didn't see anything about an arrest, did you? The investigation is still underway."

"It is? Gosh," said Minoru, sounding like a little boy. "I just knew Tokoroda from the Internet. I haven't got a clue about his private life. I didn't know him that well."

"No?" Takegami asked quietly. "Even though you referred to him as 'Dad'?"

Minoru's eyes widened slightly. Then, as if to cancel out that reaction, he blinked several times rapidly in succession. "That was just a screen name. The screen name he used."

"And you used your real name, 'Minoru'?"

"Yup. Right upfront."

"That's not common practice, is it?"

"I don't like trying to pretend."

Behind Takegami, Tokunaga's eyebrows shot up again. This time the boy apparently noticed, squinting his eyes at Tokunaga as if to size him up. "Wiseass," he muttered, before returning his attention to Takegami.

"Look, Officer, like I said, I barely knew the guy. I met him on the Internet, and we pretended to be father and son. That's it. I never had any chance to know the real him."

"We're looking for any information we can get about Mr. Tokoroda. Real or otherwise."

"Yeah? Far-out." Minoru pursed his lips. All sign of tension was now gone. He was getting into the swing of it.

"Oh, puh-leeze."

Distracted by the murmur, Chikako looked at Kazumi. "Pardon?"

Kazumi gestured toward the two-way mirror with her chin. "Why can't he use more appropriate language? He's talking to a police officer, for heaven's sake!"

Chikako smiled. "He's probably nervous. Putting on an act to cover up."

"That officer's going awfully easy on him, too. Not yelling or pounding the table."

"If he took a hard line from the start, they wouldn't be able to have a normal conversation, would they?" Chikako glanced down at the forms in front of her. "Anyway, Kazumi, what do you think so far? Does this fellow Minoru Kitajo look at all familiar? Compared to the people you saw at the station and in the parking lot—"

Interrupting her, Kazumi said flatly, "Can't tell yet. It's way too soon. I haven't seen the others yet, either."

"Fair enough."

Kazumi leaned forward, putting her face close to Chikako's. "Listen, are you positive he was my dad's Internet friend?"

Chikako looked over at the interrogation room. Takegami was rubbing his upper lip with his index finger. Minoru was laughing for some reason. "Oh, yes. There's no doubt about it."

"There are two others, aren't there? Three in all?"

"Yes, but as I understand it your dad had a large circle of acquaintances on the Internet."

Kazumi pulled away, and put one hand to her cheek. "But none of the others are under suspicion, are they? Just the members of the cyberfamily."

"Maybe so."

"Then who cares about the others?" She grew sullen. "I want to know who was in his little made-up family. Especially 'Kazumi.' If you were me, you'd feel the same way, wouldn't you?"

As Chikako gave no answer, Kazumi appealed to Officer Fuchigami, who was seated near the doorway. "Wouldn't *you*? If your dad was carrying on with a bunch of strangers like they were his real family, wouldn't you be horrified? Especially if one of them had the same name as you? You'd want to know who that was, wouldn't you?"

Officer Fuchigami smiled and pretended to consider for a moment. "It makes sense. Anyway, I can see why you're so angry."

At this, Kazumi suddenly retreated. "I'm not all *that* angry."

"No?"

"No."

Looking down, she picked up the cell phone on her lap and fingered it. Chikako nodded to Officer Fuchigami with meaning, and urged Kazumi, "Pay careful attention to what happens in the interrogation room, okay?"

Takegami picked up his reading glasses with the tips of his fingers. "Tell me how you first got to know Mr. Tokoroda."

Minoru widened innocent eyes. "I never heard the name Tokoroda, not in the beginning."

"You mean he called himself 'Dad' to you right off the bat?"

"Yeah. If you want to know about that you'd better talk to 'Kazumi.' She was involved before me."

"Kazumi? You mean the person with the screen name 'Kazumi'?"

"Who else is there?"

"Mr. Tokoroda had a daughter with the same name. It's written with the characters for 'one' and 'beautiful,' and pronounced 'Kazumi.'"

"No kidding?" Minoru leaned back in his chair.

"You never knew that?"

"No clue. Like I said, we steered clear of each others' private lives."

"Well, from the record left in Mr. Tokoroda's laptop, I must say your exchanges did give the impression of being rather—no offense—bogus."

Minoru leaned forward with such force that his chair banged against the floor. "He left old emails in his computer? He didn't erase them?"

Takegami looked at him over the top of his glasses, and nodded. "That's right. There are a lot in there."

"Going back how far? How many?" Receiving no reply, he muttered swiftly, "I'll bet the guy didn't even know how to erase them." He looked at Takegami and explained, "I always figured he wasn't as computer savvy as he let on."

"He used one at work, though."

"Not the same thing. Totally different. On a company computer, other people are in charge of installation and upkeep, but on a private computer you gotta do it all yourself." Minoru craned his neck to look at the papers in front of Takegami. "So were all the emails I sent still there?"

"Looks that way." Takegami took his hand off the pile of papers. "None of it's here, though, so trying to sneak a look won't get you anywhere."

Minoru looked annoyed. "Well, it bugs me."

"What does?"

"Email's private. I don't like the idea of the police going through messages I sent to Mr. Tokoroda."

"Sorry, but it's our job."

Minoru began tugging nervously on the sleeve of his T-shirt so that the round neck stretched down, exposing his collarbone. "Is 'Kazumi' coming in for questioning too?"

Takegami did not answer.

"She is, isn't she? You gotta talk to her. She's the one who started it all."

"You mean she was the first one to make Mr. Tokoroda's acquaintance?"

"Yes. Stop with the games, will you? You know exactly what I mean. In the beginning, he wrote only to her. That went on for a good six months. Or more."

Takegami rubbed his temple with a finger, creating a pause. Then he said, "It does seem that compared with the other two, you corresponded with 'Dad' less frequently. But that alone doesn't tell us what we need to know about your part in this Internet family. What we'd really like to know is how you got involved."

Minoru let go of his T-shirt and swept his hair back. "How I got involved, huh?"

He fell to thinking, until his attention seemed to drift. Takegami was silent, but Tokunaga cleared his throat. Minoru blinked then as if drops of water had splashed on his face, and looked back at Takegami.

"Say, Officer?"

"What?"

"This is weird. What the hell has my involvement got to do with anything? You have your suspect. 'Kazumi' and I had nothing to do with the murder." His tone had changed, and he sounded more defiant.

"What about 'Mom'?" inquired Tokunaga, leaning toward the youth. "Would you say she had nothing to do with it, either?"

Minoru went rigid. "What's with him? I thought he was here just to take down what we said. Hey man, don't jump into people's conversations like that, willya? You'll give somebody a heart attack."

"Sorry."

"For crying out loud!" Minoru jerked himself to his feet. "You know what? This is really starting to piss me off. I never shoulda come. The cop who came around to my place tricked me—Mr. Nice Guy. But now that I think of it, it's been fishy from the start. How'd you figure out I was 'Minoru' anyway?"

Takegami gave him a knowing look.

"From the email address? But providers won't let on the identity of their subscribers without good reason. It'd take a lot more than the police sniffing around for them to say, 'Here you go,' and fork over the information. I mean, you'd have to have a search warrant or—"

"You're right about that."

Having brought up the topic himself, Minoru now appeared flustered. "What? You mean you actually had one? That's how you did it?"

Placing both hands flat on the table, he stood up and shouted, "I didn't kill Mr. Tokoroda! You've got no fucking reason to suspect me!"

Kazumi Tokoroda was leaning forward with one hand on the two-way mirror, gazing intently at Minoru Kitajo. Her arm was tense, the veins standing out on the back of her hand. Chikako called out to her softly: "Kazumi, back off."

Not budging, Kazumi said distractedly, "Huh?"

"You don't want to break the glass. Take your hand off, okay?"

At that the girl came to herself, sitting back up and removing her hand. A faint handprint remained on the pane. It was just about where Minoru's face was.

"What do you think? Does anything about him ring a bell?"

Kazumi hesitated, less as if choosing her words than as if she had lost their thread. One cheek twitched several times. Finally she said, "I don't know. He kind of . . . looks a little like the guy who was hanging around in front of our house."

"You saw people unknown to you behaving as if they were on close terms with your father on three separate occasions, isn't that right? What were they again? One time was in front of the house, and the other two were on the station platform and in the parking lot of the supermarket. Was that it?"

"Huh? Oh. Yeah."

"You saw your father in the driver's seat, talking to someone through the window. Or was it the other way around?"

Chikako looked down at her notes. Kazumi slid her chair closer, trying to get a look.

"No, that's right, your father was in the driver's seat. You only saw the other person from behind, and you couldn't tell if it was a man or a woman. You weren't sure of the age, either, although you didn't think it was an older person."

"I remember jeans, I think," Kazumi murmured, then added anxiously, "Did I say that before? Do you have that down there?"

"No. Clothes . . . you just said you saw a dark coat."

"Could I take a peek at that?"

Kazumi reached out an eager hand, but Chikako slid the file out of her reach.

"Sorry, this is part of the criminal investigation so I can't let you have it. Besides, Kazumi, mistakes in memory and misjudgments are nothing for you to worry about. They're to be expected."

Kazumi stretched her neck, and looked back anxiously at the interrogation room. "But if I'm wrong, it would be terrible, wouldn't it?"

"No, because your testimony could never be the sole basis for an arrest. Nobody could saddle you with that kind of responsibility. Relax."

In the interrogation room, Takegami had called for tea, and an officer was passing cups around. When Minoru had his outburst, Takegami must have decided it was time for a break. He was urging Minoru to have some tea, while he went ahead and gulped down a cup of the hot green beverage. Tokunaga let his gaze wander over to the two-way mirror, and without signaling anything to the other side let it slide idly on again.

"I just . . . I don't know," Kazumi murmured. "It's like . . . I just lost confidence all of a sudden."

"It's the same with all eyewitnesses. It's not easy, giving eyewitness testimony."

"The whole thing about seeing people with my dad . . . maybe it was all in my mind. I couldn't remember anything right away, you know? The police asked me so many times if I remembered anything unusual about my dad that I thought maybe I did. But if I hadn't been asked that particular question, I might not have remembered anything."

Chikako patted her lightly on the shoulder. "I have to tell you, some members of the team are of the same opinion."

"They are?"

"Yes, they say the only reason you were so worried about a stalker, and then remembered seeing your father with strangers, was because the police questioned you and your mother so closely, just as you said now—trying to get you to come up with anything at all."

Kazumi's shoulders fell slightly. "Really?"

"Yes, indeed. That's why some people were strongly opposed to making you go through this identification process. They felt it was carrying things too far."

"Is that right?" Kazumi looked for confirmation to Officer Fuchigami, who nodded.

"If you hadn't agreed, none of this would ever have come about. Even now, any time you want to stop, all you have to do is say the word. What do you want to do?"

For the first time that day, Kazumi's eyes swam as she searched within herself for an answer.

"Want to call it quits? Whether you're here or not, the investigation will go on, so don't worry about that. Shall we go?"

Chikako laid a hand on the back of Kazumi's chair. Officer Fuchigami started to get up. But Kazumi shook her head as if to push aside her hesitation.

"No, I'll stay a little longer."

"Are you sure?"

"I'm fine. I have to take responsibility for what I said."

"Don't tire yourself out."

"I said I'm fine," she said peevishly, and then looked up. "Really, I am."

Chikako smiled. "I understand. Then let's carry on. Looks like they've finished their teatime over there, anyway."

Takegami was polishing his reading glasses with a handkerchief. Minoru Kitajo had gone quietly back to his seat.

"Detective Ishizu," Kazumi said inquiringly, "tell me something. Is 'Kazumi' here today? She is, isn't she? When's she coming in?"

"That's up to Sergeant Takegami."

"I wish he'd hurry up and call her in." Kazumi turned to the two-way mirror and said in a low voice, "I want to see her. Would you tell him that over the microphone, please?"

From: Minoru
To: Kazumi
Subject: cut the crap

my what a good little girl we are. cut the crap. who the
hell do you think you are?

From: Mom
To: Dad
Subject: Thank you

Thank you for this morning's email! It put a smile on my face all day.

You know, sometimes I wonder how we ever got to be family this way. I don't understand it, but it makes me happy. I knew about making friends on the Net but the thought that I might be able to have a *family* had never occurred to me.

Oh, I got a message from Kazumi before — we switched to a chat room for a while and talked. It seems she and Minoru have had another quarrel. Moderating your children's quarrels is all part of parenting so I tried to comfort her, but I wish sometime you'd sit down with each of them and hear what they have to say.

I hope work didn't tire you out too much today. See you tomorrow.

8

Takegami returned the reading glasses to the bridge of his nose and said, "Now, the four of you didn't just correspond on the Internet, you also got together in person, isn't that right? I believe it's known as meeting offline, or 'in 3-D.'"

Minoru Kitajo did not answer immediately. Having blown off some steam, and protested, and been placated, he was now back to keeping a weather eye on Takegami, watching cautiously to see what moves he might make. Eyes fixed on the tabletop, he answered with a question of his own.

"Use the Internet much, Officer?"

"I have an email address. I'm no expert."

"You sound like you were up cramming all night."

"Why, did I get it wrong?"

"No, it's not wrong. And yeah, we got together offline once. The four of us. For a family council."

"When was this?"

"Early April. The third or the fourth. The first Saturday in April."

"Saturday, April third. And three weeks later, Mr. Tokoroda gets murdered. That must've come as a surprise."

Minoru grunted, his mouth twisting into a grimace. "You bet it did. What do you expect? This may come as news to you, Officer, but I had nothing whatsoever to do with that murder. It surprised the hell outa me. Blew me away."

After this heated reply, he looked up guardedly, checking Takegami's expression. "Don't tell me—you found out about it from Tokoroda's computer."

Takegami riffled through the file in front of him. "Since you've already met her once before, you don't mind if I call 'Kazumi' in, do you?"

"Here? Now?"

"Is that a problem?"

"No, but—"

"Remember what you said before? That if I wanted to know how the four of you came together online, I should ask her. But she might be uncomfortable in here on her own."

"A regular softie, aren't you?"

"Yeah well, you two are both minors, after all," Takegami responded with a deliberate grin.

Tokunaga picked up the interphone and relayed the message, and there was an instant knock at the door. A uniformed officer entered first with a folding chair, which he set down close to Minoru. Minoru slid his chair over to one side, making more room.

"Come in and sit down."

Thus encouraged, a young woman walked hesitantly into the room. Her high-heeled, back-strap sandals clicked against the floor.

Takegami's eyes widened. The girl before him looked amazingly like Kazumi Tokoroda.

No, on second thought, when it came to details neither her face nor her figure bore any great resemblance to the other girl. Closer examination left no doubt that this was a different person. But the aura was similar. Clothes that made the most of feminine curves. Makeup that was for all Takegami knew expertly applied but still, in his view, excessive (especially considering she was seventeen, just a year older than the real Kazumi). A shoulder-length curtain of light brown hair. Even the necklace she wore was similar. It could even have been the identical item—maybe this design was all the rage among teenage girls.

A strong scent of perfume filled the room.

"Please sit down," Takegami said, and then quickly turned aside and sneezed.

Minoru Kitajo burst into a humorless laugh. "Better ease up on the perfume, doll."

The girl did not laugh back. She stood stock still, clutching a small black nylon knapsack to her chest like a shield.

"Ritsuko Kawara?" Takegami addressed her mildly. "Thanks for coming. Go on, have a seat. Don't worry, you've got nothing to be afraid of."

Something in the way he said this must have sounded funny, for Tokunaga gave a little chuckle.

The tension in Ritsuko Kawara's eyes eased. "Hello," she said in a near-whisper, the simple word sounding oddly out of place, and finally sat down.

Takegami introduced himself. Then, starting off again with, "I'm sure you've already had this explained to you," he outlined the reason for her presence there.

Ritsuko set the knapsack on her knees. Lacing her fingers nervously, she spoke up as if to push Takegami's words aside. "I'm really sad about Mr. Tokoroda getting killed. But you have to understand, I don't know the first thing about it." She spoke in a rapid undertone that contrasted strangely with the strong self-assertiveness of her attire. "I can't bear being summoned to the police station like this . . . I mean, we didn't do anything wrong." As she spoke, her hands fluttered constantly, as if to catch the words as they came out of her mouth and ball them up like tissue.

"I'm sorry you had to miss classes to come in," Takegami said politely. "We wanted to hear from all three of you as quickly as possible, and the other person was not able to get away this weekend."

"The other person?" The pair said this in unison, as if on cue. But their subsequent comments differed significantly:

"You mean 'Mom'?"

"Is that bitch coming here too?"

"'That bitch?'" repeated Takegami.

Ritsuko darted a reproving look at Minoru, who scowled back at her with evident annoyance. "Get off your high horse. You know you can't stand her, either."

Ritsuko stiffened.

"You think she did it, don't you?" he went on. "That bitch. You sent her that email. She came crying to me afterwards. I had a helluva time with her, too, let me tell you."

"What are you talking about?" Ritsuko blinked furiously. Her eyelids, covered in bright blue eye-shadow, were trembling.

Minoru raised the corners of his mouth in a sardonic smile. "You came right out and asked her, didn't you? If she did him in."

(Did *you* kill him?)

Ritsuko Kawara cried out, "No! That's not it!"

Kazumi Tokoroda jerked forward with such force that her chair jumped. Chikako reached out automatically and laid a hand on the chair back.

"Oops, sorry," said Kazumi. "I guess we shouldn't make any noise, huh?"

"No, that's all right. We can rattle around in here all we want and they won't hear a thing."

"Oh, good." She brushed a strand of hair away from her mouth, then tilted her head to one side in consideration. "So that's 'Kazumi.'"

"Yes, apparently."

"Her real name's completely different. Why'd she go and call herself 'Kazumi'?"

"I'm sure they'll get to that."

In the interrogation room, Takegami was seeking to calm Ritsuko as she waved her hands, shrieking. She was insisting on going home, that instant. Minoru threw his legs out to one side in evident disgust and glanced balefully at the two-way mirror. For a second his eyes held Chikako's, before sliding on.

"What a prick," muttered Kazumi, with such hostility in her voice that Chikako could only wonder where it came from.

Takegami managed to persuade Ritsuko to return to her seat. She wiped her face with her hand. Tears shone in her eyes.

"She's faking it," pronounced Kazumi. "She figures all she has to do is boohoo and she can make any man do what she wants. Men are just stupid enough to fall for it, too, every time."

"Not here, they aren't," put in Officer Fuchigami in a gentle tone. But Kazumi was not to be dissuaded.

"I wouldn't be too sure. Policemen are just like any other men. I bet they have their guard way down, too."

"You could be mostly right," conceded Chikako. "But I don't think you need to worry about Sergeant Takegami."

"Why's that?" Kazumi gave Chikako a sharp look.

"He has a daughter. College-age, I believe. So I'd say he has a pretty good understanding of feminine wiles."

"He couldn't, no way. What are the chances he really understands his own daughter?"

Chikako stayed silent.

In the interrogation room, Takegami was finally verifying Ritsuko Kawara's name and address, the name of her school, and other details of her identity. Kazumi took it all in, eyes intent on the scene; then she suddenly sprang to life, groped for her cell phone, and began again to make swift movements with her thumb.

Chikako looked at Officer Fuchigami. The younger policewoman steadily returned her gaze.

"You both seem a bit upset." Takegami cleared his throat. "I'm sorry but, ah, please try to calm yourselves. Maybe we should have picked a different place, after all. Just because this is an interrogation room, you must not assume that you are suspects in the case. It's just that in order to find Mr. Tokoroda's murderer, we need to learn as much as we can from people who were close to him before his death."

Minoru Kitajo crossed his legs sulkily and swung his foot. Ritsuko Kawara had wiped away her tears and sat tense-faced, clutching the knapsack on her lap.

"All right. Now, Ritsuko," began Takegami, as the girl gripped the knapsack even tighter, white-knuckled. "Minoru here says that you were first to make friends with Mr. Tokoroda on the Internet—is that correct?"

Ritsuko shot an accusing glance sideways at Minoru. Then she gave a tiny nod.

"Approximately when and how did you become friends? You haven't been going online long, have you?"

Takegami waited quietly for her to answer. Ritsuko's mouth stayed firmly shut. Just as he was about to rephrase the question, she spoke up.

"About a year ago I got a new computer."

"Your parents bought it for you?"

Ritsuko swept back her light brown hair and shook her head. "It wasn't really mine. My mother got it for herself."

"Oh? Is she a computer buff?"

"Hardly." Ritsuko dismissed the notion offhand. "If you ask me, she just did it for show. She probably wanted to brag, and let on like she knew all about the Internet. That's the way she is. Always has to be one step ahead of everybody else."

"But if she only got started a year ago, wouldn't you say she's a bit of a late bloomer as far as the Internet is concerned?"

"I know. I'll tell you what it was—one of Mother's friends had a homepage about gardening, and Mother wanted to set up her own rival website. Isn't that childish? Anyway, she tried it for a little while, but as soon as she found out how much work it is to set one up and keep it going, she quit."

"And so the computer fell into your hands."

Ritsuko nodded. "My friends told me what fun it is to surf the Net."

"How so?"

"What do you mean?"

"What do you do, exactly? Look up subjects you're interested in, that sort of thing?"

"I never really thought about it. I just go poking around different homepages—kind of like flipping through the pages of a magazine, I guess. But it's way more fun than a magazine, because there's *movement*. It's not just words on a page, it's real people, interacting with each other. Of course, to begin with, any time I logged on to a bulletin board or entered a chat room, all I did was lurk."

"Lurk?

Minoru explained disdainfully, "That means reading what other people post, without posting any messages yourself."

"I see. In that case it *would* be like reading a magazine, wouldn't it?" Takegami nodded. "Do you have a cell phone?"

Ritsuko answered yes, and then eyed him warily. "What difference does that make?"

"Well, call me old-fashioned, but to my mind girls and computers don't mix, somehow. It seems to me if you wanted to send emails and such, you could do that just with your cell phone nowadays."

Ritsuko smiled as if to say oh, is that all you mean. "Cell phones cost way more to use. If I use my computer, my parents pay the bill, because it's there in the house."

"Are your parents strict about how you spend your allowance?"

"God yes! They're a real pain. And *stingy.*"

Ritsuko Kawara lived with her father, a company employee, and mother, a full-time housewife. She had no brothers or sisters. From this, Takegami had assumed she was a spoiled only child with more money than she probably knew what to do with, but apparently he'd been wrong.

"Stingy, huh. Must be rough paying for clothes and accessories out of your allowance, then."

"Oh, that's different. If I go shopping with my mother, she'll buy me pretty much anything I want."

"Mighty generous of her."

"Well, she's always going shopping for herself, so she can't very well tell me not to. And sometimes she wears my clothes."

"Really?"

"Yeah. She's always going out, and ensembles are expensive."

"What about the outfit you have on now? Did she buy that for you, too?"

Ritsuko glanced down briefly at her attire. "Yes, except for the necklace."

The necklace just like the one worn by Kazumi Tokoroda.

"Is that a popular style of necklace?"

"This?" Ritsuko held up the chain and let the pendant dangle. "Who knows? I haven't the foggiest. I just saw it in a department store and liked it, so I bought it."

"I see," said Takegami, linking his fingers and touching them to his chin. "Getting back to what you were saying before—you were lurking on sites. What made you finally decide to post your own message?"

For some reason, Ritsuko looked over at Minoru, as if seeking his counsel. What could she want to ask? He seemed oblivious to the question in her eyes, staring only at his foot.

"Movies," she said.

"Movies?"

"Yeah. I found a bulletin board with lots of movie fans, and I liked the atmosphere—everybody seemed friendly—so I posted a short note. I like movies a lot."

"When was this, about?"

"A couple of months after I started playing around on the computer, I guess."

"That would make it about last June. Ten months ago."

"Would it?" Sounding unsure, Ritsuko looked over at Minoru again, as if to seek confirmation. This time, even he noticed.

Takegami pursued the matter. "Has Minoru got something to do with it?"

"What? No! What makes you say that?"

"Well, you keep looking his way," Takegami said reasonably, and smiled. "Is there something you won't know unless you ask him?"

"Nah, that's not it," snapped Minoru. He indicated the girl with his chin. "It's just her personality. Wishy-washy. The kind who can't fend for herself."

"That's not—" Ritsuko seemed to crumple before their eyes. She began fidgeting with her knapsack again. Minoru Kitajo glowered at her, a look of near-hatred in his eyes. Then, with an exaggerated sigh, he turned to face Takegami and explained,

"It's a homepage for movie fans called Cinema Love Island, okay? The webmaster isn't in the movie or TV business or anything, he just loves going to special screenings. You know, like they're always advertising on radio and TV: 'One hundred tickets to be given away by lottery.'"

"I've heard of it. You send in one of those postcards they have in the back-seats of taxis."

"Yeah, that's it. This guy loves doing that, and attending free screenings. He wins a lot. Must be some knack to it. Anyway, then he posts early reviews of the latest movies on his homepage. Says what the screening was like, and this and that. It's not all that interesting, but he keeps it up to date and it's pretty handy, so a lot of guys go there to check it out. Or to post their own comments."

"I see."

"A site like that doesn't attract people who are heavily into film theory, so you can relax and talk about TV movies or video rentals or whatever." Minoru Kitajo leaned back in his chair and recrossed his legs. "I used to log on sometimes, too. I know how she met up with 'Dad' there, but you'd probably rather hear about that from her than from me. Everything has to come out in proper order—right, Officer?"

"Right," agreed Takegami, and then asked Ritsuko lightly, "Mind telling us? From what Minoru just said, it sounds as though you and Mr. Tokoroda met on Cinema Love Island. Is that right?"

"Yes. . ."

"Come off it. Quit squirming and playing at Little Miss Perfect," said Minoru acidly, giving her a rough jab with his elbow. The knapsack started to slide off her lap, and she caught it with one arm.

"I'm not!" she said, her voice smaller than ever. "But . . . I'm afraid if I tell the truth they'll be shocked, and think I'm weird."

"Nothing much shocks us, and we don't go around labeling people weird," said Takegami with equanimity. Then, seeing the anxiety in her eyes, he twisted all the way around to face Tokunaga, and said, "Isn't that right?"

"Generally speaking," replied Tokunaga.

"Self-conscious Little Miss Perfect," taunted Minoru in a low singsong.

"No need to be so nasty," said Takegami reprovingly. "How do you think that makes her feel?"

Seemingly reassured by this support, Ritsuko let go of the knapsack, sat up straight, and drew her chair up to the table, shortening her distance from Takegami by seven or eight inches.

"Officer, did you see the movie *Katyusha's Love*?"

Takegami had not seen it. "I don't catch many movies."

"Neither do I, in theaters. I saw this one on satellite TV. It's a Chinese movie. It wasn't distributed very widely and hardly anybody went to see it, but after the director's next film got nominated for an Academy Award, they showed it on TV."

"Guessing from the title, it sounds like a love story."

"It is in part, but the real theme is family. The main character is a young woman living in Shanghai. Her boyfriend's mother dies and leaves her a beautiful hairpin as a keepsake. The mother'd been dead set against her son marrying this girl, but even so for some reason she leaves her this hairpin she'd had ever since she was young, that really meant a lot to her. The girl thinks this is strange, and she and her boyfriend start looking into the mother's past. Then they find out she wasn't his real mother after all, and decide to track down his birth mother."

"Interesting."

"Eventually they find out that the hairpin originally belonged to his real mother. There's a lot more, but in the end, the mystery is solved of why the dead mother was so opposed to their marriage."

Ritsuko said all this in one breath, then paused and placed a fingertip by her lips. Takegami could see the pretty manicured nail, covered in pale pink polish.

"That was the first Chinese movie I ever saw. It really moved me. I mean— it made me think about my own parents, you know? About how every mother and father was young once, and how nice it would be if their kids knew what they used to be like. I'd never thought about anything like that before. About what it was like before I was born, or what kind of lives my parents had before they got married, or anything."

"You go shopping with your mother often, though—don't the two of you talk?"

Ritsuko shook her head firmly. "Never about anything like that. Never about anything serious."

Words were coming to her easily now.

"It's always been that way. The three of us live together, but we don't have anything to do with each other. My dad's really busy and never home, and my mother's all wrapped up in her own affairs. She'll talk to me about fashion or movie stars, superficial stuff like that, but never about anything important. It was the same when I was applying to private high schools. Instead of taking the entrance exams, I applied for admission based on recommendations, but she just left the whole thing up to my teacher to decide. If I went where he thought I should go, that was fine with her.

"Sometimes I'll try going to her for advice when I'm feeling low, or when I've had a run-in with a friend, right? But she never really listens. She gets this bored look on her face. The only reason she's strict about how I spend my allowance is because it comes out of her household money. For example, suppose I get a present from a friend. Even if it's expensive, once she knows someone gave it to me and I didn't buy it, all she says is, 'That's nice, dear.' That's why at home, I'm always alone. And it's not only me. My father's alone, too, and so is my mother."

"Do your parents get along?"

"They never quarrel. But that's only because they couldn't care less about each other. That movie, *Katyusha's Love*, set me to thinking. It made me realize for the first time that there must have been a time when my parents were in love, and I wondered what that could have been like. They don't care about me now, but how about when I was a little baby? What's my family all about, what am I to my parents . . . all that sort of thing."

She'd poured out those thoughts on the bulletin board at Cinema Love Island. And had quickly gotten a number of replies, she said.

"I found out for the first time how exciting it is to say what you think, and have people respond to what you say, not just brush you aside. It gave me a thrill to think people would take seriously something I'd given passionate thought to, and think about what I said with just as much passion." Ritsuko's eyes were shining.

"I wrote all kinds of things I'd never told anyone before, about how uncaring my parents were and how lonely I was. And people wrote back to me about that, too. Some people recommended different movies for me to see, or told me not to give up even if I was lonely now, and—oh, it was so great. . ." Her face had brightened at last.

"And you used the screen name 'Kazumi' right from the start?"

"Yes. From the very first."

"Why that name, in particular? It's on the plain side for a screen name, isn't it?"

"It was the name of my best friend when I was little. Written with the characters for 'peace' and 'beauty.' Her family moved away to Osaka when we were in the fourth grade."

"You just liked the name?"

"Not only that." Ritsuko thought hard. "No . . . it was more. She was everything I ever admired. When I was little, I wanted to *be* her. She was really terrific. Sweet and cute, and lively, too. Everybody liked her. And when I went over to her house to play, her mother would be so nice to me!"

Minoru snorted. "What'd I tell you? Her head's in never-never land."

Takegami continued, "So there wasn't any deeper reason why you picked the name 'Kazumi'?"

"No."

"It's sheer coincidence that Mr. Tokoroda had a daughter named Kazumi?"

Ritsuko opened her eyes wider, and gave a firm nod. "Yes, totally. Funny, isn't it? That coincidence is what started it all."

As "Kazumi," Ritsuko had opened her heart on the bulletin board of Cinema Love Island and in chat rooms. About her lack of self-confidence, the dreariness of school, the superficial nature of her friendships, her lack of a best friend. Her lack of a boyfriend. Her fears for the future. Her sense that the emptiness of her life was irremediable.

She'd written that she had no one to talk over her anxieties with, that she and her parents were only growing further and further apart. Her father was indifferent, her mother cold. Her mother treated her like a friend, sure, but only because that was easier, and because it suited her to do so. There was no intimacy. Nowhere in the world had she ever found real intimacy.

"I don't belong anywhere—I wrote that I'd always felt that way. A lot of people wrote back to comfort me, or scold me, or give me advice."

One of them, she said, had been "Dad."

"'Kazumi, this is your dad'—that's how it started out." Suddenly, unexpectedly, Ritsuko's eyes misted with tears. "He went on, 'I just found out lately that you've been logging onto this site. I read your postings with surprise. I never knew anything about you before, and I see now how lonely that made you feel, and . . . I'm sorry.'" Her voice quavered slightly. The effect seemed contrived. "That's what he wrote. I was so happy, I could have cried."

Takegami filled one cheek with air, taking this in. "You were overcome with emotion. Okay. Why was that, exactly? Because you thought it might be a message from your real father?"

"No! I never thought that for one second."

"Never?"

"Never. Things like that just don't happen on the Net."

"Is that true?" Takegami asked Minoru Kitajo. "It seems at least possible that a parent and child could run into each other accidentally—why couldn't they?"

Minoru looked pained at such ignorance. "For one thing, unless they knew each other's screen names, they'd have no way of telling even if they did."

"But he's announcing himself straight out—'This is your dad.'"

"Anybody could write that. And as a matter of fact, he *wasn't* her dad, was he? It was Mr. Tokoroda all along."

True enough. But Takegami couldn't get rid of his doubt. If she'd never for the slightest moment entertained any notion that it might be her own parent in communication with her—if that possibility had never entered her thinking—then why react to that message with such strong emotion?

"I see what you're saying, Officer, but you've gotta figure that on the Internet, basically anytime somebody comes right out and says they're so-and-so from real life, it's crap."

"That's true," chimed in Ritsuko. "That's why that first letter from 'Dad' caused such a stir. A lot of people were upset with him for playing a mean trick on me. Or they'd send me unsolicited advice, telling me not to take it seriously or get mixed up in some game of make-believe."

Takegami said pointedly, "But you didn't listen."

She admitted it freely. "That's right, I didn't pay any attention to what they said."

Detective Tokunaga interjected a question: "What did you write back?" He wore a look of deep interest.

Ritsuko answered smoothly, with evident pride. "I said how happy I was that he understood and accepted me, and that from now on I'd tell him everything, and be the best daughter in the world. Or words to that effect." She seemed almost in a trance.

Minoru grimaced with even greater distaste than before. Tokunaga looked back and forth from one to the other, enjoying the contrast in their expressions.

"And that's how you became father and daughter on the Internet," he said.

"Yes. Isn't it marvelous?"

"Didn't it strike you as too good to be true?"

"What difference would that make? Whether such a thing could happen in real life or not, to me it was marvelous. What's wrong with that?"

"Nothing . . . but only a few minutes ago you were shaking, afraid we might think you were 'weird,' remember?"

Ritsuko drew up short and shot Tokunaga a baleful glance. "That's because I didn't want you getting any strange ideas about me."

"Oh, was that it?" he answered.

"Yes. Look, you're here to write down what we say, aren't you? Why don't you just sit back and mind your own business?"

My mistake, he mouthed, with a wry smile.

Takegami removed his reading glasses, carefully polished the unclouded lenses and replaced them on his nose before inquiring, "I'm sure the other members of Cinema Love Island didn't appreciate having you ignore their well-intentioned advice, did they?"

"Well, a lot of people did give me a hard time, but it was none of their business."

"I see."

"'Dad' and 'Kazumi' were father and daughter. On the Internet, anyway, I'd found a dad. The kind I'd always dreamed about. Why should I let perfect strangers give me grief about that?"

She'd found a father figure who would listen to her woes and respond with sincere advice, demonstrating understanding and tenderness; one who would always put her happiness first; one who expressed all this, moreover, in beautiful phrases.

But that "Dad" was, himself, another perfect stranger.

"I told them all to butt out. And that was that."

"They all figured she was a hopeless case," said Minoru, indicating Ritsuko with a careless jerk of his thumb. "They figured, okay kid, you want to play your silly game, go right ahead."

All at once, Ritsuko's smile changed to a smirk as she looked into Minoru's eyes. "The others, maybe. But not you."

Minoru humphed and made a face, then abruptly straightened his legs.

Before he could speak, Ritsuko beat him to the punch, telling Takegami, "It wasn't two weeks after 'Dad' and I started writing to each other that he came along and said he was my kid brother, Minoru."

9

For a moment, the room was perfectly still.

"I just thought I'd have a little fun," Minoru growled. He squared his scrawny shoulders, folded his arms, and began jiggling his leg. "She was really into the father–daughter thing, and wrote all this stuff that just set my teeth on edge. So I decided to mess with her."

Ritsuko was laughing. "You liar! You know you were jealous."

"Jealous? Who's jealous!"

As Minoru half-started up out of his chair, Takegami swiftly held up a restraining hand. "Let's keep our voices down, okay?"

Minoru looked at Takegami's palm, then at his face; suddenly he seemed to cool down, and settled back in his seat. "Sorry."

"Nothing to apologize for. As long as we can talk things over calmly, everything's fine. That goes for you too, Ritsuko."

Ritsuko wiped the smile off her face. She stood up and ostentatiously moved her chair away from Minoru.

"So it's correct that you introduced yourself as her younger brother, Minoru, of your own free will?"

Minoru let a few moments go by before nodding in reply.

"And that was at the Cinema Love Island site too?"

". . .Yes."

"You posted it on the bulletin board?"

"Uh-huh."

"What'd you write?"

Ritsuko opened her mouth, so this time Takegami stretched out a hand to shush her. Minoru creased his smooth forehead in a frown and stared at the table awhile before saying in a low voice, "Something about a movie that was playing. 'Cause they'd written about going to the movies together."

"'Kazumi' and 'Dad,' you mean?"

"Yeah. I dunno what movie it was. De Niro's latest. Can't really remember. I forget the title." Minoru stretched his shoulders. "I wrote, 'You two are all lovey-dovey but what about the rest of the family? . . . you're forgetting about me, Kazumi's kid brother Minoru' . . . something like that."

"And how did they react?"

"You know . . . 'Hey, Minoru!'"

"I wrote, 'You know perfectly well we invited you, and you refused to come,'" said Ritsuko. "And 'Dad' wrote, 'Well, well! You're here too, Minoru?' Then the three of us entered a chat room. A lot of people followed us, out of curiosity."

The sudden appearance of a new character must have roused the other members' interest.

Takegami asked Ritsuko, "Is that how it happened?"

"Uh-huh. But he's wrong about the movie. It wasn't De Niro, it was the one Kevin Spacey won the Academy Award for."

Tokunaga spoke up again. "That would be *American Beauty*."

"Right! You like movies, Officer?"

Ignoring this, Tokunaga said only, "It's the story of a family breakdown."

Takegami continued, "So the two of you actually saw *American Beauty* together?"

"No, no," she sighed. "You still don't get it. Back then I didn't even know who he was."

"Then wasn't it hard to write about seeing movies together?"

"No, we just played along with each other—you know, got on the same wavelength. The day before, he'd mailed me about having gone to see *American Beauty*. I hadn't seen it yet, but I knew about it from magazines. So I just made something up and sent it off to him. And based on that, he posted a message on the Cinema Love Island bulletin board, saying he'd been to see it with his daughter." A scornful smile played over her mouth. "See, it's not hard at all."

Not hard, but not altogether comprehensible, either.

"So neither of you was particularly surprised when someone popped up claiming to be your little brother?"

"Well, I kind of was, but 'Dad' wasn't."

"How could you tell?"

"I couldn't, at first. Mr. Tokoroda told me so himself later on."

"At the family council?"

"Uh-huh. After he started pretending to be my father, he figured that sooner or later other members might jump on the bandwagon. He said he thought that'd make it more interesting, because big families are more fun." She looked over at Minoru. "You were there. Remember him saying that?"

Minoru said nothing. After a pause he murmured, "I start out to bug you, and end up getting dragged into a mess like this. What a dope."

"You're not a dope," she said, suddenly solicitous. "You're just lonely.'

Minoru turned to one side and made a sound of disgust. Takegami heard him, but not Ritsuko, apparently. She went on feelingly:

"We're all lonely. We can't get people in real life to understand who we really are, and we ourselves lose sight of who we really are, and we feel alone. We want to make a connection. That's why you came to 'Dad,' looking for what your real-life dad couldn't give you. It wasn't about teasing me. All your tough-guy talk doesn't fool me."

Minoru Kitajo looked up and turned his head to look at Ritsuko. His pale brown eyes gleamed, lit by a ray of sun from the window. "You know what? That kind of talk . . . more than anything else in this world . . . is what I really . . . *really* . . . can't stand." He spoke in a jabbing style, breaking up the sentence for emphasis. "Who I really am? Give me a break. That's not why I go on the Net. You're dreaming. You're a dork."

Ritsuko was unperturbed. She wore a pitying look. "I don't mind your tough talk. You're so lonely you can't help it. I can tell. And that's why even after we met offline and I found out you were the same age as me, I went on thinking of you as my kid brother."

And still do, she murmured in a heartfelt tone.

Suddenly Kazumi Tokoroda cried out in pain. She gave the fingers of her right hand a close examination. "Oh no, my nail broke!"

Chikako took the girl's hand in hers. The long nail on her little finger had broken off at the end. Her nails were carefully shaped and manicured; probably she wore polish ordinarily, but now the nails were bare and fragile-looking.

"You can't leave it like that. You need to trim it."

Officer Fuchigami was starting to get up, but Kazumi shook her head. "I don't want to cut it. Could I have a Band-Aid? I'll just cover it up for now."

Officer Fuchigami quickly slipped out of the room. Chikako looked through the two-way mirror and saw "Kazumi" and Minoru going at it. He was giving her a piece of his mind, and she had the exact look of a bossy elder sister delivering a lecture to her kid brother.

"I hate it when you get that know-it-all look on your face."

"You need to learn to listen."

Holding her jagged nail to her mouth, Kazumi Tokoroda studied the pair. It seemed to Chikako, watching, that the emotions being vented by Minoru and "Kazumi" were reflected in their eyes. But Kazumi Tokoroda was different. Her eyes merely reflected back the light from the mirror, and nothing else. As she observed the two act out the roles of brother and sister, her gaze was mute.

"Well, what do you think?" Chikako said softly. "Notice anything in their gestures or facial expressions that seems familiar? As you compare them with your memories, is there anything that clicks?"

Kazumi said something in a small voice, her profile turned to Chikako. Unable to catch what she said, Chikako brought her ear closer. "What?"

". . . He looks like one of them." Kazumi pointed to Minoru and repeated in an undertone, "He looks like the guy in the supermarket parking lot."

Chikako shuffled through the pages in front of her. "You didn't actually hear their voices, is that right? It was pretty far away."

"Right. But I saw the way he gestured, and the way he held himself while he was talking. He did something like this before, remember?" Kazumi put both hands flat on the table and made as if to stand up. "He kind of leaned forward and hunched down, and yelled."

She imitated Minoru's posture as he'd raised his voice to Takegami, yelling that the police had no reason to suspect him of murder.

"When I saw that, I knew it was him. That's just the way someone looks talking through the window of a car, you know?"

"Uh-huh."

"When did I say I saw them talking together in the parking lot? I forget." Kazumi tried again to sneak a look at the papers in front of Chikako. Chikako gently prevented her, and countered, "Does it matter?"

"Well, the whole point is whether it was before or after their first offline meeting, isn't it?"

"The whole point . . . ?"

"Sure. If what I saw happened before the four of them got together face-to-face and found out each other's true identities, then this Minoru is lying. That would mean he'd known my father before that meeting ever happened."

"True." Chikako nodded. "In that sense, time is an important factor in all your testimony about seeing your father in the company of strangers. That's very true."

Kazumi frowned. "Then don't just sit there, hurry and check it, why don't you!"

To this outburst Chikako replied soothingly, "Yes, but Kazumi, for all three incidents, you were able to remember what you saw but not exactly when you saw it, you said. It must have been confusing to have to dredge up everything at once."

"I did so say when I saw it. I know I did."

"You said sometime in the last six months . . . so yes, you did give us a rough estimate."

"I was way more specific than that!"

Officer Fuchigami came back in and handed Kazumi an adhesive bandage strip. The girl was apparently too involved in her exchange with Chikako to do more than take it in her hand and make a fist.

"Kazumi, dear," said Chikako, laying a hand lightly on the girl's shoulder. "Don't worry too much about things. It's our job to connect the dots. Today, all we want you to do is tell us if the people in that room resemble the ones you saw with your father. Take a good look at them, and listen to their voices, and see if that triggers any new memories. That's all."

Kazumi shrugged off the hand on her shoulder. She pulled the backing off the bandage, and began to wrap it around her broken nail.

"I'm so sorry," said Chikako. The words slipped out of their own accord, a sincere expression of her feelings.

Kazumi looked at Chikako. The bandage was wrapped clumsily around the tip of her little finger, giving it an awkward shape. "Why are you apologizing to me?"

"It wasn't a good idea to put you through this."

Kazumi flinched, and averted her eyes. "I'll be fine."

"I know you will. You have what it takes. But it's painful. It would be painful for anyone."

On the other side of the two-way mirror, now Minoru Kitajo was looking sulkily away as Ritsuko Kawara spoke animatedly to Takegami, gesticulating, without looking back at Minoru.

"The heart is something you can't see with your eyes, Officer," she was saying. "When people get together, all they can see is each other's faces. Outward appearances. Real heart-to-heart connections go beyond that. But guess what? If I'm laughing, my friends and my parents think it means I'm having a great time, that's all. They never see that I'm hiding my real self, trying to fit in . . . pretending to think the same thoughts as everybody else, pretending to feel the same way they do . . . No one ever sees the lengths I go to. Nobody ever looks at me as a human being. I'm just scenery. But on the Internet I can open up my heart, and be understood for who I really am. . ."

Reading glasses perched on the bridge of his nose, Takegami was listening intently to this impassioned speech.

"Ooh, I hate her type," said Kazumi.

"What type is that?"

Kazumi pointed at "Kazumi." "The type that's always going on about 'heart-to-heart connections,' and 'who I really am,' and crap like that. It's unbearable."

Chikako smiled. Kazumi did not smile back, but perhaps she took the detective's smile as a sign of concurrence, for the line of her profile softened slightly.

"That 'Kazumi' is the same kind of person as my dad. No wonder they hit it off. They probably agreed on more things than he and I ever did. It all makes sense now."

"But for a long time you were angry about that, weren't you? About his making a pretend family on the Internet, I mean."

"Why wouldn't I be? Is there anything funny about my being angry?"

That, thought Chikako, was the sincerest question she had heard yet from Kazumi.

"My mom's not angry. That's so typical. When she found out about the pretend family, you know what she said to me? 'Your father's been lonely. There must have been a great deal on his mind that he couldn't tell me or you. I just wasn't able to see it.'" The girl's imitation of her mother was dead-on. She even had her mother's facial expressions down perfectly. "I thought she was crazy. Like, how could anybody *be* so gullible? Now, is that funny? Is there something funny about my reaction? Tell me, Detective Ishizu—am I a cold person?"

The "Kazumi" on the other side of the two-way mirror was laughing now, still talking. The Kazumi on this side watched her with clear, mirror-like eyes, her cheeks unsoftened by any smile.

"You know what? I'm absolutely certain that if my dad had lived, he'd have seen to it that sooner or later my mom and I found out about his other little family. As if to say, 'See what I've been doing, see how lonely I've been, and all because my wife and daughter wouldn't pay me any attention.' That was his theme song. Chat rooms and email may have been new, but he'd pulled the same kind of stunt before. Only the props were different."

Chikako asked gently, "You're calling what he did a 'stunt'?"

Kazumi's answer was swift and unhesitating. "Yeah, because it was. I know all about his little stunts, believe me."

As a sixteen-year-old girl?

"I know about Dad's thing for young women, and the affairs he had non-stop, one after another. It all comes down to the same thing. He couldn't live without stirring up dramas all the time. He had to play his little games in order to feel alive.

"When I was a little girl, he really loved me. I was his treasure, and he treated me like a princess. So I was crazy about him, of course, and he looked on me as his darling daughter. Beautiful, huh? That's what he really loved— not me, his actual daughter, but the *idea* of a beautiful father–daughter relationship. So long as I stayed little, and didn't have any ideas of my own, he doted on me. As if I were a cute little doll.

"Did my mom tell you this? I'm pretty sure he toned down his playing around back then, when I was little. She has to have noticed. Not that it'd occur to her to draw any conclusions from a thing like that. I don't know if he deliberately picked someone like her to marry, or if she originally had a mind of her own and he managed somehow to tame it." Kazumi raised her eyes to the ceiling, and clenched a fist in evident impatience. "But I'm different. I swear to God, I'll never be a doormat like her. How could I ever go along with his selfish little games, anyway? But he didn't like that. All he wanted was for me to stay his sweet little pet. To listen to him and grow up into just the kind of daughter he wanted me to be."

"What kind of daughter was that, do you think?"

In answer to Chikako's question, Kazumi shot out an arm and pointed to the figure beyond the two-way mirror: Ritsuko Kawara, whose fervid speech was starting to wear a little repetitious.

"Someone sappy like her. Someone always going on about finding her real self, or wanting love and understanding, or needing a place to belong. Someone who couldn't stand to be alone, who'd cling to him. Unfortunately, I didn't turn out to be a clingy, whiny weakling. I may have been his daughter, but I refused to be his ornament. I wouldn't stand for it!"

In Takegami's earphone came the sound of Chikako Ishizu's voice: "Okay if we take a short break? Kazumi seems tired."

He held up a hand to silence Ritsuko's flow of chatter. "I understand what you're saying," he told her. "Now I'd like to get back on track, if that's all right with you."

"What do you mean?" she pouted. "I *am* on track. This is all about our 'family' and how we—"

"Okay, okay. Anyway, let's take a break. The police station may not be the most hospitable place in the world, but I think we can manage a cup of coffee or so. Anyone thirsty?"

Kazumi ignored the handkerchief held out by Officer Fuchigami, instead fishing around in her knapsack for a packet of tissues. These were the first tears she'd shed since coming to the police station.

"Sorry I got excited and raised my voice like that."

"It's nothing. Don't think anything of it." Officer Fuchigami glanced through the two-way mirror into the other room. "Once things settle down over there, shall I go get you something to drink? What would you like? You like diet Coke, don't you?"

Kazumi gave a little laugh. "I can get a diet Coke here?"

"Why not? We do have a vending machine, you know." Chikako smiled back.

By the time Officer Fuchigami set off on her errand, Kazumi's tears had dried. Some of her eye shadow had rubbed off, but she made no move to repair her makeup.

"Kazumi, do you have any plans or dreams for the future?"

"Why?"

"No reason. You just seem so together for a girl your age. I thought you might have something in mind."

After thinking a moment, Kazumi answered, "In the future . . . what I really want is to be independent."

"Get a job of some kind?"

"Yeah. I'd like to be financially independent."

"A lot of young women think that way now, I guess."

"Not in your day, huh?"

"Well, back then a girl's choices were awfully limited. I just happened to end up like this. I didn't set out to be independent, like you. I had to go out to work for family reasons."

"You're lucky. That sounds so much easier. I'm jealous." After letting this admission slip out, Kazumi laughed. "Who knows, maybe if I'd been born in your generation, none of this would ever have happened."

None of this? None of what? Chikako did not ask the question. She kept Kazumi from noticing that she'd deliberately avoided the issue: "Surely there's nothing wrong with a woman becoming aware of her potential and setting out to be financially independent. It's something you can only do in this day and age, isn't it?"

Kazumi shook her head. "No, I don't mean that. Not the striving for independence, but something way more basic. I mean, in the old days, women didn't have to go to the trouble of worrying about things like that and choosing how to live, did they? You said it yourself—you ended up like this by chance."

Choosing how to live. No, Chikako had never had that luxury. But neither had she ever thought to hear someone of her daughter's generation tell her enviously what an easy time of it she'd had.

"I just don't want to end up like my mother." The girl made this cruel pronouncement in a flat, throwaway tone. "Someone who latches on to one man and hangs on for dear life, like a parasite. Living in a fog, no life of her own. I couldn't do that."

"Have you ever talked to your mother about that?"

Kazumi's eyes grew large and round. "No! I could never say a thing like that to her face."

"Because it would be a direct insult?"

"Well, wouldn't it?"

"Maybe you only think it would be. Maybe your mother has her own way of looking at things."

"Fat chance," Kazumi scoffed. "If she'd ever had the tiniest ability to look at things for herself, she wouldn't have put up with him cheating on her over and over and over like that."

It always comes back to this, mused Chikako. Kazumi's rage, Kazumi's pain.

"My dad was always lecturing me, making out like he was so much wiser than me. But he never stopped to think what he was doing to my mom— what a terrible betrayal it was. And she just kept quiet and stayed with him. What the hell's *wrong* with them, I used to think. It's beyond me."

"Well, children often have trouble understanding what goes on between their parents."

Kazumi's eyes cleared a little. "She said something like that to me once."

"Who, your mother?"

"Yes. He was behaving so outrageously, I told her she should get a divorce . . . I must've been fourteen."

"And you already knew about your father's cheating?"

"Of course. It was obvious from his attitude. And besides, women made calls right to the house."

"What did your mother say when you told her that?"

"That children shouldn't tell their parents to divorce, that my father had a lot of wonderful qualities, that they were husband and wife and no one knows what happens in a marriage except the two people themselves." Kazumi nibbled the finger with the bandage wrapped around the tip. "I remember thinking gee, I don't really want to know."

Chikako smiled. "You were too young to get what she meant."

"What? That I'll understand someday when I get married myself?" Kazumi closed her eyes in evident disgust. "Well, I don't get it. I really don't. I don't want to, either. I'd never marry a man like him, anyway."

This was of course a one-sided claim on the girl's part, a youthful conviction based on the strong assumptions of a still pure and sensitive soul. Even making allowances for that, Chikako was forced to a certain conclusion. The unhappiness of the three Tokorodas—Ryosuke, Harue, and Kazumi—had at its core a hard fact, one never spoken aloud: parents and children are not always compatible, and where differences are irreconcilable, ties of blood can end up turning into heavy chains.

Given time, perhaps those shackles could be eased and a proper distance maintained, enabling parents and children to live together without mutual hurt and distress. But for the Tokoroda family, time had run out.

Poster: Dad   09/18   00:19
Title: This is your dad

Kazumi, this is your dad. Surprised? Believe it or not, it's really me. Yesterday I happened to find out you'd been logging on to this site. You can imagine how surprised I was.

You must have met a lot of nice people here. That's why you're able to open yourself up with such total honesty. And now I've learned how you really feel.

Kazumi, I can only apologize for the way things have been between us. I never understood what you were going through until now, not once. From now on I want us to talk more, and build a better relationship. Can you forgive me? Will you accept my change of heart?

10

As Chikako knocked on the door and opened it, Harue Tokoroda looked up. Her eyes were red; she'd been crying. She was clutching a handkerchief.

"How's it going?" asked Chikako, as gently as possible. "Have you had a chance to look through everything?"

"Yes." Harue nodded and stood up, swiftly dabbing at her eyes with the handkerchief. "I'm sorry to take such a long time. It's just brought back so many memories. . ."

The articles that had been a messy heap on the table were neatly organized. Haruo must have done that as she examined them one by one.

"I sorted out my husband's personal belongings. The things that should go back to the company are over here." She indicated the right half of the table. Some sort of cord was included in the pile. Picking it up, she mumbled, "I don't know what this is for. . ."

"Looks like a cable for computer accessories."

"Oh, right."

"Your husband owned a laptop computer. You know about that, don't you?"

"Yes. But it's not here."

"I'm sorry, but we still have it. To return just the cable when we're holding on to the computer shows somebody here is either awfully scrupulous, or just plain senseless." Chikako grinned ruefully, and Harue's mouth relaxed into a smile.

"I don't know the first thing about computers," said Harue. "I'm terrible with any kind of machine. My husband tried to teach me, but I was hopeless.

Of course, he never used to know anything about computers, either; the younger men at work were always showing him what to do. That hurt his pride, so he made up his mind and studied up on the subject."

Minoru Kitajo's comment flashed through Chikako's mind: "I always figured the guy didn't know half as much about computers as he let on."

"Did he take classes somewhere?"

"Oh no, nothing like that. He bought a lot of books, and for a while he was up late every night, staring at the computer screen."

"About when was this?"

"Let's see . . . a couple of years ago, it might have been."

Harue turned her eyes to the tabletop and picked up a book from the pile of things to be returned to her husband's office. Judging from the cover, it appeared to be an introduction to the Internet.

"This has the stamp of the General Affairs Department in it. Looks like he borrowed it and never returned it."

"Well, that sort of thing happens."

Harue carefully laid the book back down on the table. "I wonder if I could trouble you for a paper bag or a cardboard box," she said.

Chikako promised to get something for her right away. "Did anyone come by while you were here?" she asked.

"A woman brought me a cup of coffee . . . Why?"

"Oh, no reason. I just hoped no one bothered you, that's all. The other thing is, I'm terribly sorry but it looks like we're going to need to keep Kazumi here a while longer. What would you like to do? Do you want to wait?" As she asked, Chikako looked deep into Harue's eyes. What she wanted to know most of all was whether, when she looked straight into her eyes like this, Harue would dodge her gaze.

Harue did not look away. Her eyes shone with nothing but a mother's concern. "Is it all right if I wait?" she asked.

"Of course. I'll find some place more comfortable for you."

"I don't mind staying here. I need to pack up his things anyway. It's just . . ."

"Yes?"

"Is Kazumi really being of any use in your investigation?"

Chikako motioned for Harue to sit down. The grief-stricken mother lowered herself back into her chair, feeling her way with her hands.

"You've been worried about that all along, haven't you? But remember what I told you before: valuable as her testimony is, we have no intention of putting the burden of proof solely on her shoulders. We would never—"

Harue interrupted, shaking her head. "I know, I know. I understand. It's just . . . You know, I—I hardly know how to put this. It's a fine thing for a mother to say, I suppose. . ."

Harue's emotions were clearly seeking an outlet, struggling to find a way out of her body in words. Chikako waited.

"As I was sitting here this morning, turning over everything in my mind, all at once I lost confidence in what she's been saying all this time."

"You did?"

"Yes. The idea that she saw my husband with some sort of strangers—not just once, but several times . . . I just wonder if she isn't mistaken. You know, acting under a false impression. After all, she did turn out to be wrong about the stalker, didn't she?"

Chikako nodded slowly. "I see. So that's what's on your mind."

"With that business about the stalker, we had extra police protection at the house, and I felt terrible about it afterwards. Now with this business . . . if it were just a question of Kazumi giving testimony about what she saw, that would be one thing, but to have these other people brought in and interviewed in front of her . . . to have all of you go to so much time and trouble, if it turned out to be all in her mind again, I just—I wouldn't know how to apologize."

"Please don't worry about that, Mrs. Tokoroda. It's our job to clear up every point of doubt, one by one, no matter how small. That's what we do." As she spoke, Chikako looked again into the depths of Harue's eyes. Again, no sign of duplicity. Only the emotions contained in her words were reflected there, and nothing else.

Mothers are sad creatures. The thought swept over her. *We mothers are sad. Left behind. Left out.* The emotion was overwhelming. Words pushed up as far as her throat, but with an effort she swallowed them back down.

"I'll go look for something you can use to pack his effects in." With this, she got up. Filled with bitter self-loathing, she stepped quickly out into the corridor to keep Harue from noticing anything amiss.

When the interphone rang, Minoru Kitajo and Ritsuko Kawara both jumped. A chill came over Takegami at their too-sensitive response.

Detective Tokunaga picked up the phone, spoke a few words, and looked at Takegami. "Gami, over here."

Takegami had assumed the call was for him, but quickly realized that Tokunaga was instead asking him to step out of the room.

"We'll leave you two in here on your own for a while," he said lightly. "That'll be more relaxing, right?"

Minoru said sardonically, "You'll be keeping an eye on us anyway. Who do you think you're kidding?"

As Takegami left the room, Ritsuko was saying in a low voice, "Keeping an eye on us? What do you mean? Then we *are* suspects?"

Once outside, Tokunaga gestured down the corridor. Takegami followed behind him double-time, and just around the corner they ran into Detective Akizu, standing blocking the way.

"Oh, it's you."

Akizu opened a nearby door, shoved Takegami and Tokunaga into the room, then hurriedly closed the door. It was a storage room, the narrow space crammed with a jumble of supplies.

"What the hell's going on?" Takegami demanded, then blurted out the thing uppermost in his mind: "Has there been a change in Naka's condition?"

"No, nothing like that. No change there," Akizu hastened to reassure him. "It's something else."

"They found it," said Tokunaga.

"Found what?" asked Takegami, eyes narrowing.

"The millennium blue parka."

Akizu glared at Tokunaga. "Hey—quit stealing my thunder, willya?"

Who gives a damn about that? Takegami measured his breathing. "Where?"

The heavyset Akizu looked down at Takegami and said solemnly, "About six hundred yards north of East Koenji Station, there's a bowling alley that went bankrupt and shut down. Kamikita Bowling, it's called. The parka was in a garbage dump out behind it."

Takegami drew a mental map. East Koenji. Bowling alley.

"The place shut down three months ago, but you know how it goes —there's been trouble with creditors. The building's been sitting there abandoned with the dump piled high with all kinds of junk from inside. This morning the contractor finally started to clean it up—"

And what should turn up but a bright blue parka. Akizu indicated his own chest and abdomen. "Apparently the thing's plastered with blood. After all this time it must have gone putrid, and probably stinks to high heaven. At first the workers just stood there with their mouths hanging open, but after a minute somebody remembered about the Suginami case. They called us right away."

"So far it's just the parka?"

"Yeah. The forensic team took off already."

"Is the dump easily accessible from outside?"

"It's just behind the bowling alley, marked off with an iron fence. I'm sure you could easily toss something in."

Takegami nodded slowly.

Tokunaga crossed his arms and said, "The timing is pretty amazing. There's no saying how this may all turn out yet, but don't you get the feeling that somehow Nakamoto's persistence paid off?"

Takegami rubbed his chin.

"What do you want to do, Gami?"

"It's not up to me to decide."

"You're sounding faint of heart." Akizu's nostrils flared. "That's not like you."

"I'm a coward from way back. What about Shimojima?"

"He was glued to the phone when I left. How're things in the interrogation room?"

"We're on a break. Akizu, get Ishizu over here. I think she's with the mother, in the first-floor conference room. I'll talk to Shimojima."

"Righto," said Akizu, and strode off. Takegami and Tokunaga stepped out of the utility closet, too.

"You go back to the interrogation room," said Takegami. "Don't tell them anything. No need to say anything to Fuchigami yet, either."

"All right."

"Don't let them out of the room. I'm counting on you."

"Don't worry."

Takegami headed back to the briefing room. Halfway up the stairs, he encountered Officer Fuchigami hurrying down. She called out to him.

"I heard the news already," he said. "Where's Shimojima?"

"In the chief's office."

Seated in the immaculate office were not only Police Chief Tachikawa and Captain Shimojima, but Captain Kamiya as well. The first words out of Kamiya's mouth echoed what Tokunaga had said before.

"The parka turning up this way is a tribute to Naka's persistence. We owe this to him."

"It seems a little too good to be true," responded Takegami. "Things are going according to plan otherwise. . ."

Shimojima was relaxed. "How does it look?"

"Can't say one way or the other yet."

Tachikawa cut in. "Then it's *not* according to plan. You've had a good two hours in there. Now that we have the parka, we could call the whole thing off."

"If having the parka in hand changes the situation, we might as well call it off," said Takegami, and then countered, "How's Miss A taking it?"

"We haven't told her yet. Since the forensic team went out, the reporters have probably gotten wind of it, but this is an in-between time of day." It was nearing three P.M. "If we want to keep it quiet awhile longer, we've probably got till the evening news. This isn't a big enough piece of news for the networks to interrupt their regular programming."

"She may hear about it from the reporters hanging around her."

"We could always let that happen and watch her response. In any case, the thing came out of a garbage dump, right? Even if we can analyze the bloodstains, the chance of getting any hair or fingerprints is probably zilch. We might be able to trace it right to the buyer by using the product number to track the distribution route, but that takes time."

Ignoring the others, Shimojima addressed the chief. "Unless Miss A breaks down on hearing the parka turned up, and starts confessing, nothing's changed in our case against her."

Hearing that, Takegami was relieved. Shimojima was for going on with the plan.

"East Koenji—does she have any familiarity with that area?"

"The name hasn't come up in any of our investigations so far. You haven't turned it up, either, have you?"

"No. Is it all right if we introduce the discovery of the parka?"

The chief started to say something, but Shimojima was faster. "Absolutely. That's bound to have a quick effect."

Deep creases appeared in the chief's forehead. "Too risky. Even if you do get positive proof that way, after the indictment there'll be hell to pay with the lawyers."

"We're not using deceit, so that shouldn't be a problem. It's perfectly true that the parka was found."

"Yes, but—"

"What we're after is a confession. No—more than that. We want a surrender." Takegami spoke quietly. "Superintendent Kasai approved the plan on that understanding."

"I don't need to be told that."

"Our chances of getting what we're after have increased enormously with the discovery of the parka. Please let us carry on."

Chief Tachikawa's face reddened. "We still haven't ruled out Miss A—how can you be so damned sure of yourself?"

"Of course there's no positive proof at this stage. All the more reason we need to straighten this out."

"Please listen to him."

The voice came from the back of the room. Everyone's head swung around at once. Chikako Ishizu was standing in the doorway.

"I beg your pardon. I knocked, but no one heard me."

"What's Mrs. Tokoroda doing?"

"She's decided to wait for Kazumi."

"Good thing we detained her."

"She's extremely anxious." Chikako looked at Takegami. "I heard about the parka. I agree that we ought to proceed quickly, and see what we can find out. Please allow us to continue."

Takegami and Chikako both bowed their heads in silent entreaty. Even if they did have the approval of the investigation commander, to proceed over the objections of the police chief was unthinkable. It could only lead to trouble later.

Tachikawa grumbled, "This amounts to an undercover operation, you know that." That much had been clear from the start; no point in raking up that debate again. Takegami and Chikako kept their heads lowered.

"Well, I guess it won't do to leave it half-finished," said the chief weakly.

"Certainly not," Shimojima assured him.

"If nothing comes of it, we press ahead with Miss A. Is that clear?"

Chikako breathed a sigh of relief. Takegami looked at his watch. 3:15 P.M. About time they ended the break; Tokunaga must be sweating by now.

When they stepped into the corridor, Captain Kamiya asked crisply, "Gami, have you contacted Torii?"

"Not yet. No word from him yet, either. I told him to stay glued to his post till the last possible minute."

Torii was Takegami's junior colleague, a detective in the Fourth Squad headed by Kamiya.

"When the parka news comes out he'll need backup. Handling a rapidly changing situation is not his forte."

Torii, though a good man, was a bit inflexible. That tendency had gotten him into trouble on several past cases. He was well aware of his own weakness, however, and earnest about changing, so Takegami had gone ahead and given him this chance.

"Shall I send Akizu?"

"He's chafing at the bit, but he'd only destroy Torii's credibility. I'll go," said Kamiya decisively. "That's the quickest way to handle it."

Takegami gave a slight laugh. "Might be a waste of your time."

The corners of Kamiya's mouth turned up. "You seriously mean that?"

"No. But just half an hour ago, I had my doubts. Frankly, if you look hard at the facts, I still don't know whether I buy into Naka's theory or not."

"You sounded pretty optimistic in front of the chief just now. That's our Gami. Who else could mix such optimism with such caution?"

"You know, I have to second what you said before."

"About Nakamoto's determination?"

"Think about it. The parka we hunted for and never found all this time . . . suddenly it turns up, and at such a critical moment. Hard not to feel there's an invisible hand at work."

"Could be." Kamiya nodded, and smiled wryly. "But we learned in training that obsession leads to false charges—remember?"

"It's ten years since my last training session," said Takegami. "But I'm still learning plenty from Nakamoto."

The captain clapped him on the shoulder and said, "I'll be in touch." Then he took off.

"Shall we be on our way?" urged Chikako Ishizu. She was wearing her motherly face, but something in her gentle smile bore a reminder of the past.

From: Mom
To: Dad
Subject: Thanks for last night

Thank you for taking me along to check out the new house last night. It felt as if we were really going to look at our own house — I was thrilled. I hope we can sell off the old house and work out a way to pay for the new one before long, don't you?

You know, I think all my life I've been lonely. Things probably won't change from here on, either. That's why it means so much to me to know you and to share experiences like this with you.

I'll stay out of your life as much as possible, and I won't cause you any trouble, so please include me whenever you can.

11

When Takegami returned to the interrogation room, Ritsuko Kawara was laughing hilariously. Minoru Kitajo wore a look of bitter disgust. With that expression on his face, he did not look at all like a teenager.

"Officer, this cop slays me." Ritsuko pointed to Tokunaga, who remained seated at his desk. Tokunaga's face was deadpan.

"Sorry to walk out on you like that," said Takegami. He took his place, settling the glasses back on his nose. Chikako's voice sounded in his ear.

"Are we back in business? Kazumi has requested that you get Ritsuko Kawara to lean forward and say something in a low voice. With her back turned this way, if you can manage it."

Takegami nodded, dropping his gaze to the papers in front of him.

"Okay, where were we?" he said. "So far, three people are involved in your Internet 'family'—'Kazumi,' 'Dad,' and 'Minoru.'" He looked up, comparing the two faces before him. "So the three of you would travel around from site to site on the Net carrying on conversations, in character, everywhere you went—but there was more to it than that, wasn't there?"

"What're you asking *us* for?" Minoru retorted sullenly. "If you've been through Tokoroda's computer, you know what we did. Why do cops always ask questions they already know the answer to?"

"We sent email back and forth, and we made a family bulletin board just for us, and we chatted, too," said Ritsuko. "Had online conversations, I mean. Mr. Tokoroda—'Dad'—set up the bulletin board and chat room for us."

"When was this?"

"When was it? You tell, Minoru." She leaned over. "I can't remember."

Minoru stared into space, thinking. "Didn't take long to do. Musta been up and running by last October, anyway."

"And from then on, Mr. Tokoroda managed the service for you?"

"Yeah—but I don't think it cost him any money. There are plenty of free providers."

"So in a sense, the Internet provided your 'family' with a home."

"Right. Nicely put."

"Now tell me how 'Mom' joined in."

For some reason Ritsuko hung her head and fell silent, stealing another sidelong glance at Minoru. Paying no attention to her, he lifted his eyes and looked levelly at Takegami.

"She wandered in by chance one day."

"Oh?"

"Yeah. Somehow or other she stumbled on the family bulletin board—I think she was doing a search with 'family' as the keyword. Around the end of the year. Christmas." Minoru shrugged his thin shoulders and added harshly, "Why not just ask her yourself? She's here, isn't she? Stop beating around the goddamned bush."

"A point well taken. All right, I'll ask her to come in then, shall I? You'd rather stay here for it, wouldn't you?"

"Um, Officer. . ." Ritsuko was showing signs of nervousness. "Like Minoru said, I did suspect her of being the murderer. . ."

Takegami waited in silence.

"Right after Mr. Tokoroda was murdered, I got an email from her saying something terrible had happened to him. That was literally the first thought that went through my mind. It was such a shock. . ." Her voice trailed off.

"So you sent her a return email asking, 'Did you kill him?'"

Ritsuko winced. "When you say it straight out like that, it sounds atrocious."

"I don't think it's atrocious, but it is fairly intense."

"That's what I'm telling you—the words just popped out. . ."

"We weren't getting along too great." Minoru Kitajo jumped in swiftly, as if in her defense. "Things were awkward. Had been all along. You know that, too, right? If you've been reading his email you must know that much."

"We did notice that you had the least share of the correspondence," said Takegami, checking his notes. "Let's see. We've seen all his mails, starting with the one he sent 'Kazumi' last January fifteenth at ten P.M., and ending with the one he sent 'Mom' on April twenty-sixth, the day before his murder, during the noon hour—probably on his lunch break. . ."

"If you say so," said Minoru with a shrug.

"Mr. Tokoroda corresponded frequently with 'Mom' and 'Kazumi,' but not much with you, Minoru. The number of exchanges with you goes down every month."

"I got tired of it," said Minoru simply. Then he added, "Unlike *her*, I didn't run crying to the Internet because my life was in the toilet."

"Neither did I!" said Ritsuko, incensed.

"Tired of it or not, you still showed up on April third, though, isn't that right?"

"That was our first family council. Our last, too, as it turned out. Yeah, sure, I went. I was interested. Curious. Wondered what they all looked like in 3-D. So I went."

Takegami gazed steadily over the tops of his glasses at Minoru Kitajo's face. Minoru began to look uncomfortable. He recrossed his legs, rattling his chair against the floor as he did so.

"For now," said Takegami, "I'm going to ask you two to leave the room for a while. I want to talk to 'Mom' and get her side of the story. I'll call you back in right away. Mind waiting in another room for a couple of minutes?"

Ritsuko grimaced. "If we're not here, God knows what harebrained story she'll come out with."

"Well, we'll give a listen to whatever she's got to say."

Takegami made a phone call and had the two escorted from the room. Minoru went out first, dragging his feet a little. Ritsuko Kawara was following him out when Takegami called her back: "C'mere a minute, will you?"

With the table between them, he signaled to her until she bent down towards him, and then he said softly, "Answer me in a low voice. Are you afraid of Minoru Kitajo?"

Her eyes widened momentarily, and she whispered back, "Yes, a little."

"Do you think he had something to do with the murder?"

"Gee, I—"

"While you're in the other room, I don't want you talking to him. There'll be an officer present at all times, so don't say a word."

"All right."

She nodded and quickly left the room, as if fleeing.

Chikako looked at Kazumi's profile. The girl was studying the two-way mirror intently, with her chin drawn in and her lips pursed.

"That rings a bell," she murmured. "I'm starting to think she's the one I saw in the supermarket parking lot."

"Not Minoru Kitajo?"

"No. About the person I saw on the station platform, I'm not so sure. I could be way off base there—it might have been someone harmless from the neighborhood. Dad was active in the neighborhood association, so he knew a lot of people."

"Kazumi."

For a moment, the girl appeared unaware that her name had been spoken. Her face was blank. Suddenly her eyes lost their intensity, and then she turned to Chikako.

"What?"

"Aren't you getting tired?"

"Me? No." She swept her hair out of her eyes and said flatly, "I'm fine. I'll see it through. Tell him to hurry and call 'Mom' in there."

She groped in her purse and fished out a hairbrush. At the same time, her cell phone fell off her lap. Quickly she snatched it up and held it tight in her left hand. Then she began brushing her hair with hard, jerky movements, as if angry.

Watching, Chikako said in a matter-of-fact tone, "You've been cooped up in here all afternoon—Tatsuya must be wondering where you are."

Kazumi's hand stopped moving. After a beat, she answered, "He sent me an email before."

"Oh, so that's why you answered right away." Chikako smiled. "I guess an email from your boyfriend is enough to make anyone a bit fluttery."

Kazumi finished brushing her hair without speaking, and then began pulling loose hairs from the hairbrush and letting them drop at her feet. She did it with an air of long habit.

"Doesn't he work in the daytime?" asked Chikako conversationally.

"In a convenience store," said Kazumi shortly.

"Wasn't it a gas station?"

"That was before, when you were staying with us. He changed jobs since then."

"Oh, really? I heard you make more money at a convenience store if you work the night shift."

"Yeah, but he's got another job at night."

"At a pub, if I remember right. A pretty hard worker, isn't he?"

"He has to save money. He wants to go into business."

"That I didn't know." Chikako turned and looked at Officer Fuchigami, who smiled. "Did you?"

"I'd heard about it. He wants to open a coffee stand, isn't that it?"

Kazumi put away the hairbrush and crossed her legs. "He'll run a franchise at first. He needs the experience before setting up on his own. He has to raise money for the security deposit."

"Will you help out?"

"I mean to eventually, but first I have to go to college." Kazumi fingered her hair impatiently. "Anyway, that's all beside the point, isn't it? Let's get started."

From: Ryosuke Tokoroda
To: Yoshie Mita
Subject: Sorry

I'm awfully sorry, but could we put off our appointment for the day after tomorrow? How does a week after that sound—sometime around April 30?

I really hate to do this after the trouble you took to contact me. Sorry.

12

"Please have a seat," said Takegami.

She appeared to be in her mid-thirties. A slender, demure woman, dressed primly in a pale green suit. Light makeup. At her throat, a pearl brooch. She looked like a mother dressed for her child's school entrance ceremony.

"Thank you."

Sharp chin, small eyes, pale lips. The overall effect was not unattractive.

"Yoshie Mita?"

"Yes, that's right."

"Your address is . . . let's see here . . . Saitama Prefecture, Tokorozawa City. . ." As he read out her street address, the woman nodded in agreement.

"And you live alone?"

"Yes, I do."

"You're not married."

"No."

"You work for Chizuka Electrical Parts—is this the address of the head office?" he asked, indicating the form in front of him.

"Yes, that's the head office in Tokyo. I work in the General Affairs Department."

Utterly unlike Minoru and Ritsuko when they had first entered the room, she spoke with the poise of an adult. Her voice was rather low, but the words were distinct. She gave the clear impression of being an office worker used to dealing smoothly with clients over the telephone.

"What sort of work does your department do?"

"We handle things like employee vacations, overtime pay, and company housing."

"I see. So basically your work involves internal affairs."

"Yes. I believe that's usually the case for any General Affairs Department." The briefest flicker of a smile crossed her face. Noting the change in her expression, Takegami suddenly felt that her makeup, unobtrusive though it was, was actually applied with utmost care and subtlety.

"How long have you worked there?"

"This year it will be fifteen years."

"That makes you an old hand, doesn't it?"

Yoshie Mita said nothing, and dropped her gaze. Her hands were neatly folded in her lap, the nails evenly trimmed. On the ring finger of her right hand she wore a ring set with a small green stone. Jade, maybe.

"Ah—" She spoke with evident diffidence. "May I confirm that I've been called in today in connection with the murder of Ryosuke Tokoroda?" She sounded exactly as if she were speaking on the telephone to a favored client or bank representative.

"That's correct."

"I'd like to know if I am a suspect in the case. Am I under suspicion of murder?"

"Why do you ask that?"

Yoshie Mita looked around. "Well, isn't this where you interrogate suspects?"

"It is, yes."

"Then wouldn't bringing someone here for interrogation signify that that person is a suspect?"

"Not necessarily."

The brevity of his answer seemed to leave her at a loss. As Takegami had been seeking to prick her composure, he counted this a success.

"When word came that the police wanted to see me, I . . . spoke with an acquaintance of mine."

"Okay."

"I thought perhaps I might need a lawyer."

"And did your lawyer accompany you here today?"

"I haven't engaged one yet. But my friend will introduce me to one whenever I want."

Takegami said nothing, only looking steadily at her face. Yoshie Mita clasped and unclasped the fingers in her lap, licked her lips nervously, and finally looked up.

"I believe I understand why you might treat me as a suspect."

"Oh? Why is that?"

Yoshie raised one hand and laid it over her heart. Then she dropped her gaze again, and began to speak in all earnestness. "I was friends with Mr. Tokoroda. We met on the Internet. Since you know about me, I assume you've already investigated our connection."

"We have." Takegami removed his glasses and massaged the bridge of his nose before continuing. "We also know that you and he were part of a make-believe 'family.'"

Yoshie Mita closed her eyes. "Then Kazumi and Minoru—yes, of course, you must have called them in, too."

Takegami said nothing.

Yoshie's hand went up again, this time covering her mouth. Holding it there, she said in a muffled voice, "They think I did it. They must have told you so."

"I haven't heard anything directly from them about that. But it is true, isn't it, that when you emailed them after learning about Mr. Tokoroda's murder, Kazumi wrote back asking point-blank if you'd killed him?"

Yoshie covered her face with her hands.

Kazumi Tokoroda's right thumb was moving briskly. She was sending a message again, her movements swift and on-target. Her expression was intense, her eyes all but devouring the cell phone.

Chikako waited for her to press the "send" button and then said, "All finished?"

"Huh?" Kazumi appeared taken aback. "Oh . . . yes. I'm sorry. Didn't want him to worry. You know."

Over in the interrogation room, Yoshie Mita's face was still buried in her hands. Takegami, his arms lying on the table, hands clasped, was looking straight at her.

"Now you've gotten an idea of what all three of them are like."

Kazumi glanced over at the two-way mirror. "She seems like the quiet type."

"She could easily be someone's mother, don't you think?"

"I guess. She's not my dad's type, but I can see how she might've been perfect for the role of mother in their little game. Of course, you can't tell what someone looks like on the Net, so I guess it didn't really matter." Suddenly she pursed her lips spitefully. "I'll bet something comes over people like her in that anonymous environment. I'll bet she acted really forward and aggressive, you know?" With barely a pause, she asked, "How long is he going to leave her like that? Is she crying?"

Takegami cleared his throat and addressed Yoshie. "Are you all right?"

Yoshie finally lifted her face, one hand over her eyes. The corners of her mouth were tight.

"I'd like to verify something, if you don't mind," Takegami went on. "You stumbled accidentally on the bulletin board that was serving the others as home, is that right?"

Yoshie nodded several times.

"Around when did that happen?"

"The end of last year—about the middle of December."

"Did you write something soon after finding it?"

"No . . . I waited for a week or so to see what would happen."

"Lurking?"

"What? Yes—just watching."

"What did you think? That it looked like fun?"

Finally Yoshie removed her hand, exposing her face. Her eye makeup was smeared. "Well, not 'fun' exactly. . ."

"What about the combination of father, older sister, and younger brother? Did you think it was real?"

"Of course not." She shook her head wearily. "I knew right away it was a game."

"How could you tell?"

"Oh, it was all just a little too good to be true."

Takegami grunted. "I don't follow you. In what way was it too good to be true?"

Yoshie drew back slightly.

"From what I've seen of the bulletin board where you all posted messages to each other, nothing would have made me think it wasn't real," Takegami said. "The individual emails are another matter. Those do sound more like play-acting, I'll grant you that."

Yoshie shrank back. "Mr. Tokoroda and I . . . we. . ."

"Save that for later. Right now I want to know what was 'too good to be true' about the interaction of those three people."

"The content of their exchanges . . . I guess that would be it."

"Can you be more specific?"

"Well, for example. . ." Yoshie looked up at the ceiling. "When 'Kazumi' wrote that her grade average had gone down, and mentioned how disappointed she was, 'Dad' wrote back immediately. His letter was sweet and understanding, full of encouragement. She'd been called in for a teacher conference, and all he said was that if they were going to be discussing her college plans, he'd like to go, too. Now I ask you—where in the world is there a father that angelic?"

"Oh, I don't know. There are a lot of types out there. I wouldn't be surprised if there was an actual father like that."

"Well, yes, there *could* be—but still." For the first time, her voice took on a tinge of irritation. "I can't explain it. You wouldn't understand unless you saw for yourself the smarmy phoniness of that message."

"Be that as it may, you were interested in them," Takegami went on, undeterred. "And you decided to step into the remaining role—the role of mother. Did you introduce yourself as 'Mom' from the start?"

"Yes."

"Without letting on that you knew it was all a game?"

"That's right."

"What did you write?"

"Oh, you know—'Well, well! I *thought* you all seemed to be having a fine time with your computers lately—so this is what you were up to! Let me join in the fun, all right?' Something like that."

"That sounds kind of phony, too, doesn't it?"

"What I'm saying is, the atmosphere encouraged that kind of phony heartiness. They took to me right away. 'Mom! What took you so long?!' That sort of thing. It was all an act. That's what was so much fun."

"More fun than real life?"

"Well, yes. Yes."

Takegami set his elbows on the table, and leaned forward. "But you met in real life too, didn't you? On the afternoon of April third, the four of you got together face-to-face for the first time. Isn't that right?"

Yoshie's cheeks stiffened.

"If you were enjoying a kind of pleasure unattainable in real life, why would you do a thing like that? Once you'd all met in person, wouldn't that undermine the fantasy aspect of the game you'd been playing on the Internet?"

Clenching the hands on her lap into fists, Yoshie twisted her lips. "We had decided—" Nervous tension made her voice rise in pitch. "—to call the game quits. That's what occasioned the get-together."

Takegami's eyebrows went up. "But the game didn't stop. The mails kept right on coming, didn't they? Mr. Tokoroda even sent one to 'Kazumi' saying the get-together had been fun and he wanted to do it again."

Squirming, Yoshie shook her head. "I know nothing about that. I did see the message 'Kazumi' posted on the bulletin board, saying how much she'd enjoyed it, but that's all."

"Are you sure it wasn't just you who wanted to call it quits?"

"Me?" She raised a hand to her suit lapel and repeated, "Me? What makes you say that?"

"You wanted to have an exclusive relationship with Mr. Tokoroda. Or, I should say, you already did. An intimate sexual relationship. Am I wrong?"

Her lips trembling, Yoshie stared at Takegami. "You know, don't you?"

"'You wanted to get rid of 'Kazumi' and Minoru and deepen your relationship with him, one-on-one. Didn't you?"

Silence.

Takegami continued relentlessly. "Ryosuke Tokoroda was a married man. He didn't have the slightest intention of breaking up his family. You knew that. You went with him to look at a new house he was planning on buying to replace his old one, isn't that right? And you sent him an email after that. You said it felt as if the two of you had been checking out a house of your own, and that you were thrilled. You remember writing that to him? Am I wrong? And the place you visited was the scene of the crime. That's where he was stabbed to death."

No answer.

"You wanted to tear down the wall between reality and the fantasy you were living out. You began to wish you could be his wife in real life. And as that intention of yours—ambition might be a better word—started to surface on the Internet site where your pretend family hung out, Minoru picked up on it, and he began to distance himself. His postings became fewer and farther between. Were you aware of that?"

Yoshie looked down, blinking hard. The rest of her face was a mask.

"And the reason 'Kazumi' wrote back asking if you had killed him was because she was aware of the part of you that could no longer be satisfied with games. Yes, they both suspect you. Until a little while ago they were sitting right here in this room telling me about it. They both think you could have killed Ryosuke Tokoroda and Naoko Imai, the girl who'd been intimate with him."

"I didn't kill anyone," said Yoshie, without raising her face. The blinking did not stop. "Of course not Mr. Tokoroda, and I never even knew about Naoko Imai."

Takegami let this defense pass. Flipping through his papers, he pulled out another page and began to question her in a leisurely way.

"Where did the April third meeting take place?"

"What?"

"The family council. Where did you arrange to meet?"

The switch to a new line of questioning seemed to fluster her. "It was . . . at the station. . ."

"The east exit of Shinjuku Station? Two P.M.?"

"Th-that's right. You must have looked this all up; you know all about it, don't you? We decided the time and place online."

"You agreed that all four of you would be carrying an Internet magazine, as a sign."

"Yes."

"But you couldn't just stand there outside the station talking for hours on end. You must have gone somewhere else after that."

"Oh, if that's what you mean . . . we went to a coffee shop."

"What was the name?"

"I don't remember. Mr. Tokoroda took us there. It wasn't far from the station."

"All four of you went?"

"All four of us went."

"And what did you think?"

"I beg your pardon?"

"Did it seem awkward to meet in person after playing 'family' together on the Internet, or wasn't there much sense of incongruity?"

"Oh, that. . ." For some reason, Yoshie nodded with apparent relief. "Actually, both Minoru and 'Kazumi' were so young that I felt as if they could really be my children."

"And Mr. Tokoroda? Did you feel he could really be your husband, too?"

Yoshie did not respond.

"Far from any sense of strangeness, you felt the two of you were a perfect fit, a very desirable fit, did you not? At least from your point of view."

"Officer, these are leading questions."

"They're not meant to be."

"Oh, but they are. You want me to say 'yes,' don't you? You want me to say that I wanted us to become lovers, isn't that the idea? It is, isn't it?"

Takegami ignored her questions. He turned to another page and asked in a leisurely way, "On April twenty-third, Mr. Tokoroda sent you an email, did he not? From his office laptop. He asked to reschedule a date to meet with you. He suggested putting it off a week, till April thirtieth."

Yoshie again grew flustered. "All right, yes, I did receive an email like that. But I don't remember the exact dates. You can't expect me to answer a question like that."

"There's something more important than the date in that communication," Takegami went on. "Mr. Tokoroda sent it under his real name, and he sent it to you by your real name. No more 'Dad,' no more 'Mom.' Just Ryosuke Tokoroda and Yoshie Mita. Now, how do you account for that?"

Yoshie sat back from the table, as if to distance herself from the question. "I don't know. It must be because we'd met and introduced ourselves to each other in person by then. I didn't pay any particular attention to it."

"Didn't you? I interpreted it as a sign that your relationship with Mr Tokoroda had advanced to a personal level."

"You're making way too much of it."

"You did have a date to meet him on April twenty-third, though, didn't you?"

Again, she said nothing.

"That wasn't another family council, now, was it?"

She muttered something unintelligible.

"What? I couldn't hear you."

"Why must I discuss any of this with you?"

Takegami changed tack again. "What was the atmosphere like on April third? Was it harmonious?"

"I thought so."

"And it was after that that you and he visited the housing site that later became the scene of his murder, is that right?"

". . . Yes. I've forgotten the date."

"That's barely a ten-minute walk from the Tokoroda house. By car or bicycle it would be only a couple of minutes away. Weren't you afraid of what you might be doing to his wife and daughter?"

"Well, it was only a weekday evening. It wasn't as if I'd monopolized him on a Saturday or Sunday."

"That's a new one on me."

"All I did was accompany him there. Mr. Tokoroda was very cautious about buying property. He went to see that one lots of different times, at different times of day. He went more than once at night. He'd stop off on his way home from work. He mentioned he was planning to go there again that day, so all I did was tag along."

"About what time? After looking the place over, you had to get from Suginami all the way back to Tokorozawa, right?"

"It wasn't terribly late. Perhaps nine or so."

"Then the two of you might have been seen by someone in the neighborhood?"

Yoshie's voice became shrill again. "What if we were? I have nothing to feel guilty about!"

Takegami fixed a calm gaze on her until the last trace of her outburst had faded away. Then he said laconically, "Shall we ask Minoru and 'Kazumi' to join us now?"

"It's weird," murmured Kazumi.

"What is?" Chikako leaned over towards her.

"Look at her. Yoshie Mita." Kazumi pointed at the woman on the other side of the two-way mirror. "She's way more suspicious than the girl that's practically been accused of the murders, don't you think? Minoru and 'Kazumi' think she did it, too. And yet nobody's picked up on it. That poor Miss A had paparazzi from the weekly magazines following her around."

Chikako followed the direction of Kazumi's fingertip. Yoshie Mita's profile was undistinguished, the line of her jaw particularly unimpressive.

"Are the police really zeroing in on her, and just not letting on?"

"I don't think there's any conclusive evidence tying her to the crimes."

"Or for Miss A, either."

"Yes, but Yoshie Mita had no connection with Naoko Imai."

"I'll bet she heard about her from my dad." Kazumi was coldly offhand. "Straight from the horse's mouth. She was alone with him, wasn't she? They went to the very place he was murdered, didn't they? He must've said something to her then."

"Kazumi." Chikako shifted her knees and turned to face the girl. Kazumi made no move to return her gaze, but continued staring at Yoshie Mita's profile. "Do you really think your father would have done a thing like that?"

"A thing like what?"

"Tell another woman that he had a girlfriend named Naoko Imai."

"I wouldn't put it past him at all." She spoke indifferently, out of the side of her mouth. "I can just see it. Yoshie Mita comes on to him, and he gets all shook up, and tells her he's already got one lover and that's all he can handle. Sure he'd tell her."

"And after hearing that, Yoshie Mita thought that if only Naoko Imai was out of the picture she could grow closer to your father, and so she killed her?"

"You got it."

"But in that case, after she'd gone to all that trouble to get him for herself, why would she turn around and kill him too?"

"Because he wouldn't have her, probably."

"You mean your father turned her down?"

"That's right. That's what I'm telling you. He liked younger women. He'd never have given anybody her age a second look." Kazumi waved a hand dismissively. "That must've driven her right up the wall. Here she thought she'd finally landed herself a man." She frowned maliciously and said in a mincing voice, "'You know, I think all my life I've been lonely.' She tried to pass herself off as Miss Lonelyhearts—and I bet she *was* lonely, as far as that goes. That's why when she thought she had a chance to get her hands on a man, even a total stranger, she went for it. No holds barred."

Chikako said quietly, "If that's true, your mother might have been the next victim."

Kazumi blinked. "What?" Now she turned and looked at Chikako.

"Well, even if she managed to get rid of Naoko Imai, there was someone else in the way—Mr. Tokoroda's wife. Your mother."

"You're right." Kazumi shrugged. The open neck of her top revealed the graceful line of her collarbone. "I guess she might've been in danger."

"Isn't that scary to think about?"

"I guess so." Kazumi averted her eyes. "Now that you mention it, what's my mom doing right now?"

"Waiting for you."

"She should go on home without me." She looked down at her cell phone. Checking the time, apparently. "It's late! Four-thirty. I'm tired. How much longer is this going to take?"

"Well, the real question is, what do you think from what you've seen of Yoshie Mita so far? Does she look familiar? Is there any resemblance between her and the people you've testified about seeing?"

A look of genuine surprise crossed Kazumi's face, as if she'd forgotten all about the task at hand. "Right, right. That's why I'm here, isn't it?" She stepped closer to the two-way mirror. "But you know, I'm not really sure about her. I kind of think now that the person hanging around our house *might* have been a woman, but maybe I only think that because I've seen her and heard her telling her story. You know what I mean?"

The girl was not only lovely to look at but quick-thinking too, thought Chikako with admiration.

"In any case, no matter what I say or don't say, if she's the one who killed my dad, I don't think she can cover it up much longer, do you? Looks to me like she's on the edge of hysteria. She could break down and confess any minute now. I thought that sergeant was just a sourface who couldn't fight his way out of a paper bag, but he's not bad, is he?"

"You mean Sergeant Takegami?"

Chikako tried to smile, but did not succeed very well. Looking at Kazumi's lips, their distinct curves one element of the girl's undeniable beauty, she was picturing the time when in a show of fierce will those same lips had let fly the words, "I'll kill whoever did it! I swear I'll get revenge!"

From: Kazumi
To: Minoru
Subject: what's up?

hey minoru what's up? i'm really depressed. have you talked to mom? she's mad at us, isn't she? i'm not talking to her. if she sends me mail i just ignore it.

it's thirteen days already since dad died. wow. i can hardly believe it. you know what i do? i mark the calendar with an x for every day that goes by without them catching his murderer. it makes me sad but otherwise it's like nothing's happened and i might slip up and send off an email to him like old times. mr tokoroda meant so much to me. he was my *dad*. i was so glad i surfed the net. didn't we have fun? is it all over now? was what I did bad?

i don't know who the murderer is but it's not you and it's not me. i'm still suspicious of mom....

write back ok? i emailed you yesterday and the day before and you haven't said anything yet.

i'm lonely and scared. i want to see you.

From: Minoru
To: Kazumi
Subject: so long

just so you know, this is my last email to you.

apparently the police gave mom a good going-over. she said it
was because you fed them a mixture of fact and fiction. she
was steamed all right but at you not me. drop the *us* ok?

mom says that when tokoroda was killed she was in osaka at
an in-house training session. as soon as that came out,
she was in the clear, but because the detectives went
poking around where she works the boss has it in for her
now and she might have to quit. she was boohooing about
that. she thought since her name never got in the papers
she'd be ok but apparently in a big company like that they
don't take kindly to police investigations.

whatever. i'm fed up with the whole thing. you following
the papers? they're back to miss A, whoever she may be.
she'll be arrested. that'll be that.

can't say i thought as much of tokoroda as you did. as a
guy i can't go along with what he was up to. i'm not just
saying that after the fact either. i've said it ever since
I laid eyes on the sob.

well I feel a little sorry for miss A. of course she's an
idiot. watch out you don't end up like her.

this is it between you and me. kazumi's little brother
minoru is history.
so long

13

No sooner were "Kazumi" and Minoru back in the interrogation room than the intercom phone rang, as if it had been awaiting their return. Tokunaga let it ring twice before picking up the receiver.

"Gami, it's for you."

Takegami got up, turning his back on the three seated on the other side of the table, and took the phone.

"Torii here," announced a voice mixed with static. "So can we talk?"

"Hey," responded Takegami calmly. "What's happening?"

They had arranged beforehand that unless Takegami said something about coming down with a stomachache, the conversation could proceed normally. Even so, Torii spoke in a cautious undertone. "Nakamoto's prediction was dead on. The boyfriend's shaking in his shoes."

"Huh."

Deep down, Takegami felt a ripple of excitement, but he answered with a noncommittal snort, feigning lack of interest. Even so, the trio looked on with apparent suspicion. Beyond the two-way mirror, what would be the look in Kazumi Tokoroda's eyes as she watched the scene unfold?

"Heard about the parka from Kamiya. The media haven't picked up on it yet. Nothing's been on the radio, so the boyfriend's probably none the wiser."

"Check."

"Your guys know yet?"

"Nope."

"Gonna tell them pretty soon now?"

"In a bit."

"If the boyfriend makes a move, I'll let you know."

"Got it."

As Takegami replaced the receiver and pulled out his chair, Ritsuko Kawara leaned forward and asked intently, "Did that have something to do with us?"

Takegami put on his glasses. "We do have other cases to deal with besides the Tokoroda homicide."

"Oh. Right," she said, deflated, and jiggled her leg like a little kid. It struck Takegami that despite the apparent casualness of her demeanor, of the three facing him she was the most on edge.

The air in the interrogation room had changed. He could feel the heavy weight of it bearing down on him, could almost feel its very texture. It was like being trapped in a wad of wet and sticky cotton. Takegami had to swim through it, somehow find a way out.

Yoshie Mita had deliberately drawn her chair away from her "children," and was sitting at an angle facing away from them. Minoru Kitajo looked her up and down; then, with exaggerated furrows in his brow, he asked Takegami, "So, did she confess or what?"

Yoshie jumped to her feet as if she'd been struck. Her expensive handbag slid off her lap and the clasp fell open, the contents spilling out. A tiny pouch . . . a cell phone . . . a notebook with a pink cover. With the mortified look of someone caught in her underwear, she hurriedly scooped the things up and stuffed them back in her handbag.

"Are you all right?" Takegami asked.

"Y-yes," she stammered.

He waited for her to sit back down and then slowly started off. "For people who haven't seen each other in a while, you're certainly thick as thieves."

No one answered.

"Now that you're all here, I'd like to share some news."

They each held themselves in a different posture to listen, ears perked.

"We've found the millennium blue parka."

Each registered surprise differently as well. Flat-out astonishment. No dissembling here.

Takegami regarded Minoru Kitajo over the tops of his glasses and went on, "You must have seen it on the news. It's an imported article of clothing which we have reason to believe was worn both by whoever strangled Naoko Imai and by whoever stabbed Ryosuke Tokoroda to death. Until now we couldn't determine if it was a vest or a parka, but apparently it was a parka."

Minoru bristled. "What are you telling *me* for?" he demanded, up on his feet.

"I'm not telling only you."

"The hell you aren't! You're looking straight at me! Women wear parkas, too, you know."

With exquisite timing, Yoshie Mita said maliciously, "That may be, but this Canadian manufacturer deals exclusively in men's garments, I happen to know."

"Who asked you?" Minoru gave his chair a kick, toppling it over with a loud crash.

Takegami remained seated, elbows on the table and fingers intertwined, making no move to intervene. It was Ritsuko Kawara who stepped in.

"Stop it! Let it go." She put her arms around Minoru and said, in a voice choked with tears, "Don't let the things she says get to you! That's just her little game."

"And that's yours," shot back Yoshie. "Playing the innocent. My, what a good little girl our 'Kazumi' is, and how she can cry at the drop of a hat."

"Kazumi" spun around and made as if to hit Yoshie. Takegami issued a hasty reprimand, adding, "The parka we found is heavily stained with blood. Mr. Tokoroda's blood, probably."

Abruptly Ritsuko lowered her arms and returned limply to her seat. Minoru picked up his overturned chair and seated himself in it with a clatter.

"Blood shed by Mr. Tokoroda," repeated Takegami. "He was stabbed twenty-four times in all, remember."

"Where . . . did they find it?" Ritsuko asked huskily.

Without a word, Takegami looked again at Minoru.

"I'm telling you, I don't know anything about it." Minoru defended himself in a more restrained tone than before. "Quit eyeballing me, will you?"

"I'm not focusing on you in particular." Takegami sat back, folded his arms, and looked at each of the three faces evenly, in turn. "Have any of you heard the expression 'evidence talks'?" he asked. "It does, and very eloquently, too. It tells us all sorts of things. Now that the parka has surfaced, this case is going to break wide open."

Someone in the room gulped audibly.

"Even so, we'd like to save ourselves unnecessary time and trouble. If any of you has anything to tell us, now would be the time." He glanced at his watch. "I'll wait three minutes."

The second hand had just passed twelve. *Good, that makes it easy.*

Silence ensued.

"Wh-why are you saying this to all three of us?" Ritsuko's voice shook. "Why lump us all together?"

Takegami's eyes were on his watch. "That's thirty seconds."

Minoru screwed up his face so much, the effect was comical. "Hang on a minute now. You think we're conspirators or something?"

"That's ridiculous!" Ritsuko cried out, pressing her hands to her cheeks. "Is that it? Is that what you've been thinking all this time? Is that why you went to so much trouble to get the three of us together again?"

"You gotta be kidding me," said Minoru. "Come on, Officer. What are you, nuts?"

Takegami never lifted his eyes from his watch. "Going on one minute."

Kazumi Tokoroda too had laid a hand over her mouth. "Is it true?" she asked, through her fingers. "Is it?" When Chikako didn't answer right away, Kazumi turned and grabbed her by the arm. "Tell me, is it true? Did they really find the parka?"

"Yes, it seems so," Chikako replied quietly. "We just got word a little while ago."

"And it's the one the killer had on?"

"Yes. Covered with blood."

Officer Fuchigami went over to the girl. "Kazumi?"

"I . . . don't feel so good." Kazumi abruptly slumped in her chair. A curtain of hair fell across her face, hiding it. "It's because you said 'covered with blood' like that."

"I'm so sorry."

"When did they find it? Have they reported the find on TV?"

"It's probably making the news right about now."

For a second, Kazumi's eyes stared into space. Then all at once, as if aware that she must not at any cost let on what it was she saw, she held her head in both hands and squatted to the floor.

"I feel sick," she groaned. "I'm all dizzy. . ."

Chikako bent down and laid a palm on the girl's back, feeling the rhythm of her shallow, rapid breathing. She would have given a great deal to see the swirl of thoughts and feelings in the girl's heart right now.

Yet Kazumi kept her wits about her. She was thinking as fast as she could, trying to help herself focus by crouching down with her face covered, her eyes turned aside. Chikako wanted to tell her that she didn't have to do that anymore. *Go on, take the easy way now*, she pleaded silently. *It's enough. It's over. This is the end.*

Perhaps a minute went by. Then all at once Kazumi shoved Officer Fuchigami aside, grabbed her purse, and stood up. "I want to go to the bathroom," she said.

"Will you be okay by yourself?"

Kazumi raised her eyebrows defiantly and raised her voice. "Don't tag along!" She was all but shouting.

Officer Fuchigami retracted her hand, startled. Seeing her error, Kazumi flinched.

". . . Uh, I'm sorry."

"That's all right. You know where the ladies' room is? Just down the corridor, around the corner on the right."

"Okay."

Heels clicking, Kazumi set off down the corridor. Her footsteps were unsteady, and one shoe sounded about to come off. They could hear her progress even through the closed door.

"It seems cruel," Officer Fuchigami murmured, eyes on her feet. Chikako was silent, waiting for the rest to come, but the policewoman let the thought go unfinished. Instead, she voiced an apology: "I beg your pardon."

"Don't be silly. I feel exactly the same way."

With that, Chikako swiftly got up and, with a nod to Officer Fuchigami, slipped out into the corridor. As she closed the door, she could hear the police-woman saying into the microphone, "Kazumi has left the room, and Detective Ishizu has gone after her."

Chikako was wearing rubber-soled shoes. Her footsteps made no noise. All she could hear was the steady, solemn beating of her heart.

Before reaching the ladies' room, Chikako halted at the storage closet and listened at the door, just in case. It was the same closet that Takegami and the others had rushed into barely an hour before. In this unfamiliar setting, it seemed unlikely that Kazumi would rush blindly behind the first door that came along. Though it was a long shot, she checked it out just to be sure. Hearing nothing, she proceeded to the ladies' room.

The lavatories on this floor were small; when you pushed open the door, the sink was almost close enough to bang into. Further in were two stalls. That's where Kazumi would be, in one of those, she thought, but just to be sure, she went ahead and checked the stairwell beyond the ladies' room. No one was there, but from downstairs, through the door on the floor below, she heard a flurry of voices. An office. With uniformed police officers coming and going, Kazumi could ill afford to risk setting foot in there.

Returning to the corridor, Chikako went and put her ear to the ladies' room door. She could make out no sounds from within of running water or of talking. Cautiously she inched the door open and stuck her head inside. Then from an inner stall she heard a voice.

"So anyway, don't worry, okay?"

It was Kazumi. She was talking briskly, in a hurry. Her voice sounded persuasive, soothing.

"You're in the store? Don't react if you see the news. I'm telling you, everything's perfectly fine. Guaranteed. Okay? Okay? So listen to me. *Please.* Come on now, get a grip. Okay?"

Her voice seemed close to tears.

"Huh? Yeah, yeah. The police are no problem, trust me. They don't suspect a thing. I mean it. They think those other people did it. Yeah! My being here has nothing to do with anything."

She was striving to keep her voice down, but her agitation was evident. *This is cruel. Was cruel,* thought Chikako. *But two people are dead. Which was crueler?* Had they failed to act, more murders might have taken place. Kazumi's nimble fingers, sending out a stream of email messages. How else could they have put a stop to her feelings of anger and hurt?

Which was crueler?

Mentally, Chikako addressed Nakamoto. Unable to imagine him lying helpless in the ICU, she pictured him instead as he had looked the first time she met him, when she was summoned to headquarters to hear his theory. *Bravo*, she told him. *Well done.* Then she stole back down the corridor, the way she'd come.

"Kazumi's talking on her cell phone." Chikako's voice sounded in Takegami's ear. "No doubt about it, it's going exactly the way Nakamoto said it would." Takegami frowned deeply, causing the three across the table to stiffen their spines. "Officer Fuchigami is stationed in front of the lavatory now, in my place. When she gets back I'll let you know."

Takegami turned to the two-way mirror and nodded. Then he said to Tokunaga, "Get Torii. Kazumi Tokoroda is on the phone."

Torii picked up on the first ring. "That you, Gami?"

"What's going on?"

"He's holed up in the back, no sign of coming out. I saw him get a call."

"It's Kazumi. Is there a back way out?"

"Don't worry, we got it covered. His picking a convenience store was a break for us. The walls are plate glass."

"Don't spook him."

"I know."

"Don't come on too strong."

"Gami." Torii's voice went down. "I learned my lesson, okay? Leave this to me."

"I'm counting on you. If we blow this now, after coming so close, I'll never be able to look Nakamoto in the face again."

Takegami hung up and wiped his face with his hand. "Am I in a cold sweat?" he asked Tokunaga.

"You're fine. You don't look any different."

"*You're* awfully calm."

"Who, me? I'm just stage equipment." He looked up at Takegami. "Naka-moto really nailed it, didn't he?"

"Seems that way."

"It's gone like clockwork. Surprising how readable they are after all. Kids today."

"That's because when all's said and done, they're still kids."

Tokunaga made a face. "Isn't this a bit like twisting a baby's arm?"

Takegami did not answer.

"That was uncalled for. Sorry."

"Forget it. The main thing is, don't let down your guard."

Takegami looked over at the threesome sitting at the table. Three pairs of eyes looked back at him, solemn and clear.

14

Kazumi Tokoroda burst back into the room with a noisy protest. Officer Fuchigami had a grip on her arm, albeit a light one, and she was resisting.

"How are you feeling now?" asked Chikako, swiftly approaching her.

"I want to go home." Kazumi avoided looking Chikako in the eye. "I said I was going, but she wouldn't let me."

Chikako put an arm around the girl and attempted to lead her back to her chair, but she put up a fierce struggle, bracing her legs. "I've had it! I can't take this anymore!"

"What's wrong, all of a sudden?" Chikako looked into her face. "What's got you so upset?"

Chikako's query, calm yet insistent, seemed finally to get through to Kazumi. The tension drained from her.

"I feel sick—like I might throw up. Let me go home." There were beads of sweat on her forehead, and her hands were shaking. "Imagining the parka with blood all over it was too much. I can't breathe. I don't want to be here anymore."

"All right, let me send for your mother. You can go home together."

"No! Never mind her!"

"I'll go and get her." Officer Fuchigami set off smartly down the hall, as if glad to get away. Some of the pain she must be feeling echoed in her footsteps. It was understandable. Inwardly Chikako sympathized, remembering the considerable time the policewoman had taken cultivating a friendship with Kazumi.

"We'll get a car and send you straight home. Just wait a moment."

Over the mike came the voice of Yoshie Mita in the interrogation room. Kazumi stood rooted to the spot, facing a corner of the room, her arms wrapped around herself.

Chikako looked over at the two-way mirror.

"Well, nobody confessed," said Yoshie, her head hanging. "Are we still under suspicion?"

"You could wait three minutes, three hours, or three days, and it wouldn't make any difference," Minoru said, jiggling his leg again. "I don't know anything about a parka. Not a thing."

"Neither do I!" said Ritsuko.

"There were other people with motives besides us, you know," said Yoshie. "Mr. Tokoroda was having problems at home." She sighed. "He said the atmosphere was icy."

"Right. So you thought he'd divorce her and marry you instead," Minoru jeered. "What a dope! Married men always say that. At your age you ought to know better."

Yoshie scowled at him. "Mr. Tokoroda didn't complain about his family just to me, and you know it! You both heard him. He went on and on about it that time we met."

"Is that a fact? All I remember are your sob stories about being alone and lonely and bored."

"*Will you stop being so obnoxious!*"

"Ooh, temper now!"

Takegami picked up a sheaf of papers and rapped them sharply on the tabletop to align the edges.

Minoru gestured with his chin. "See there? You made the officer mad."

"I want you to understand something." Yoshie gripped the edge of the table with both hands and leaned forward, addressing Takegami. "Ryosuke Tokoroda was a lonely man. I sympathized with his loneliness. I was lonely, too. Our 'family game' had meaning and worth. It wasn't just for kicks."

Minoru was shaking his head. Yoshie went on.

"He was unhappy. Things weren't going well between him and his wife and daughter. He told me his life was a sham—that he had nothing to live for."

Takegami responded quietly, "Did he say that was why he was seeing Naoko Imai?"

Yoshie did not flinch. "Yes. It's true, he had a weakness for women. But it was more as if they wouldn't leave him alone. Even at work—there'd been some sort of trouble with women there."

"You're awfully well informed."

"Well, it must have come up in the course of your investigation, didn't it?"

"We never heard about it, no. His colleagues and staff at Orion Foods are a close-mouthed bunch. No one ever said a word about anything like that."

"Blabbermouth," said Ritsuko, looking balefully at Yoshie. "You know, everything was fine till you came barging in. Did you ever stop to think about that?"

"Why blame me?"

"Because it's all your fault."

"What is? What exactly have I done? Tell me. Spell it out in words of one syllable."

Ritsuko gave a contemptuous laugh.

"Can't do it, can you? It all comes down to one thing: you're jealous."

Ritsuko's eyes widened. "Jealous? Of who?"

"Mr. Tokoroda accorded me special consideration as the 'Mom' in the family. That got to you, didn't it? It infuriated you that you weren't number one anymore."

Ritsuko elbowed Minoru, sitting next to her. "Get a load of that! Has she got a screw loose or what? Talk about deluded."

"Why, you little—" Yoshie lunged for Ritsuko, scratching furiously.

Minoru leaped up again.

Takegami bellowed, "That's enough!"

The three froze. The room became very still.

After a moment, something clattered loudly to the floor. It was Detective Tokunaga's pen. He looked around at everybody, said, "Pardon me," and bent over to retrieve it.

An awkward pause ensued. Ritsuko Kawara let out a childish snicker.

"Isn't he funny?" she said to Minoru. "He kills me."

Again a hush fell over the room. Emerging from the quiet there came the faint wail of a siren, gradually stealing closer. The sound was coming from Shibuya, headed this way. Homing in on the police station.

"What now, some other crime?" murmured Ritsuko. "Busy place. Aren't you about through with us now?"

"Yeah," Minoru chimed in. "You've got your parka, so what do you need us for? The parka's gonna lead you to the real killer, isn't it?"

Detective Tokunaga picked up the phone and spoke sternly to whoever was on the other end of the line: "What was that siren just now? We could hear it in here plain as day."

After a brief pause he said curtly, "I see," before replacing the receiver in its cradle and turning to Takegami. "They're here."

"*They*?" persisted Ritsuko. "What other kinds of cases do you handle, anyway, Officer? Is it all homicide?"

"That's got nothing to do with you," said Takegami. "Isn't the murder of Ryosuke Tokoroda enough for you? We need to stay focused on finding his killer."

Yoshie stretched out her legs in an oddly suggestive way, and said, "I'll tell you what *I* think. It's his wife." Malice dribbled from the corners of her mouth. "His wife killed him. It has to be her. I mean, weren't there reports of a woman's screams coming from the scene of the crime?"

"That's it?" said Takegami. "That's your theory?"

"Yes," she said shortly, and looked up. "Who but his wife could have hated Mr. Tokoroda and Naoko Imai enough to kill them both? I certainly can't think of anyone else."

"You can't?"

"You're sympathetic to her, aren't you, Officer? I know, he was cheating on her, so technically he was at fault. But it's never just one person's fault when a marriage goes bad."

"I'm not buying it," said Minoru. "That whole thing was Tokoroda's fault."

Paying him no mind, Yoshie directed her gaze straight at Takegami as she went on: "His wife did it. First she killed Naoko Imai and then she went after him, stabbing him over and over again. It just goes to show how distraught she was."

"If she was going to kill him anyway, you'd think she'd have done it at home."

"Not necessarily. She could have been lying in wait for him, knowing he'd stop by there on his way home from work. After she killed him, she rushed back home. It's not far. She could easily have done it."

"I see. But the only basis for your theory is her supposedly being 'distraught,' is that right?"

"No. There's a solid factual basis." A steely glint flashed in Yoshie's eye. "This came up when the four of us got together that time, so you two should remember," she said, with a glance at "Kazumi" and Minoru. "Mr. Tokoroda said he was being watched."

"Watched?" Takegami screwed up his face questioningly.

"Yes. He said that whenever he went out, he felt like someone was following him. And he was fairly certain it was his daughter."

"Kazumi Tokoroda?"

"That's right. The whole reason we had the meeting at two P.M. on that particular day was because her cram school was giving a big exam that Saturday—April third—and so he wouldn't have to worry about her following him around."

Ritsuko and Minoru looked at one other.

"Is this true?" asked Takegami.

"Yeah, basically," said Minoru.

"He did say something like that," agreed Ritsuko. "When we met in front of the station, he seemed kind of nervous, too. Said he didn't want his daughter following him around." She looked at her fingernails. "I thought to myself, God, these people are sad. Was his daughter Kazumi that twisted?"

Without responding, Takegami turned back to Yoshie. "Suppose Kazumi *was* keeping an eye on her father's movements," he said. "That's her business. I can't see that it gives any grounds for suspecting her mother of murder."

Impatiently, Yoshie said, "Don't you see? Mr. Tokoroda's wife was using her daughter to spy on him!"

"That's quite a leap."

"Then you don't understand women. Mrs. Tokoroda knew perfectly well what a cheater her husband was. Deep down she was furious, but on the surface she pretended to be charitable and forgiving. That meant she couldn't go snooping around after him herself—not when she was supposedly above such pettiness. So she got her daughter to do it for her, instead."

Yoshie sounded very sure of herself. Pursing her lips, she went on, "For all I know, the girl cooperated with a vengeance—girls always side with their mothers. And she'd been poking around in her father's laptop, too. He said he was aware of it, but he wanted to see his daughter's reaction, so he was deliberately ignoring her behavior and letting her look around all she wanted."

Takegami was incredulous. "You're telling me Kazumi Tokoroda knew all along that her father had another family on the Internet?"

With a proud tilt of her chin, Yoshie said, "That's what I'm telling you. That's why he was so careful that time we got together, for fear Kazumi, or even his wife, might come barging in. Kazumi Tokoroda knew about us, all right. And I'm fairly certain she didn't like it much, either."

"That's a lie!"

At some point, Kazumi had turned round to face the two-way mirror. She hugged herself tighter, a vein throbbing visibly in her neck.

"It's a dirty lie,"' she repeated, and shook her head so emphatically that her chestnut hair bounced and swung. "She's lying."

". . . Kazumi."

"I don't know anything! I didn't know! It's all lies, lies, lies, lies!"

"Let me get one thing straight." Takegami slowly shifted in his seat, leaned back against the backrest, and looked the trio in the face. "Ryosuke Tokoroda had a daughter named Kazumi. A real, flesh-and-blood daughter."

Minoru tightened his lips until the lower lip almost disappeared, and stared at the tabletop. Ritsuko was watching Takegami. Yoshie sniffed with disdain and turned her gaze out the window.

"Kazumi was keeping an eye on the Internet 'family' that you three formed with her father—and her father knew she was. You all heard him say so. Am I right so far?"

Ritsuko nodded.

"And even though he knew, he made no move to conceal it from her because he wanted to find out how she would react. Isn't that what you said?"

Ritsuko nodded again, and lowered her eyes.

"Also, he revealed to the three of you that his family life was not happy. That his relationships with both his wife and his daughter were frigid. That he was, essentially, alone." After a little pause, Takegami added, "To me, that all sounds like nothing but a selfish rationale for irresponsible behavior."

Yoshie finally blinked, and turned her jaw stubbornly away.

"Of course," Takegami went on, "it's a chicken and egg kind of thing. Mr. Tokoroda could have gone after other women *because* his marriage was in trouble. He could have searched the Internet for an ideal match, and then started up his pretend 'family.' Or it could be that his irresponsible behavior is what sent his marriage into crash mode in the first place. There's no telling which came first. Or maybe they both did, depending on how you look at it."

"I—" Ritsuko began to say something in a low voice, but abruptly fell silent.

"Ryosuke Tokoroda probably had no notion of the selfish cruelty he was inflicting on his wife and daughter. People never do."

"Making a pretend family in cyberspace—why is that so selfish and cruel?" asked Yoshie hotly. "We were never *really* a family to him. It was just a game of make-believe. Something that existed only on the Internet. We played at being an ideal family. Each of us enjoyed acting out our role. Was that so awful?"

Slowly, Takegami shook his head. "What you did, in itself, is neither selfish nor cruel. We can all benefit from a certain amount of fantasy in life."

"Then what's wrong with it?"

"When the fantasy starts affecting reality, it's a different matter."

Yoshie looked disdainful again, and Ritsuko hung her head even lower.

"The moment Kazumi found out about it, Mr. Tokoroda should have called a halt to the whole thing. But he didn't. Still, he had one more chance after that to put on the brakes. You know what I mean—the get-together, when he looked you all in the face and started grumbling about his real family life, even admitting that Kazumi was sneaking peeks at his laptop."

He addressed Ritsuko Kawara. "Kazumi Tokoroda is a girl just like you. Did you know that?"

Ritsuko made no answer.

"When you met Mr. Tokoroda and heard what he had to say, didn't you feel anything? No matter how phony your game of the 'perfect family' may have been, didn't you think it was wrong to rub her nose in it? Weren't you able to step back for one little minute and think how she would feel?"

"But I—"

"You said you were upset with your parents for paying no attention to anything you do, isn't that right?" Takegami pressed on. "Well, suppose that after never showing the slightest interest in you, your mother and father went out and found a complete stranger and then played the part of perfect parents to her. Wouldn't that hurt? Wouldn't you be angry? How about it?"

Minoru moved abruptly and said, "That's why I decided I'd had enough." Takegami looked at him silently. Minoru looked steadily back at Takegami, but couldn't maintain eye contact long. His gaze wandered away. "It just seemed wrong, you know?"

"Did you say so to Mr. Tokoroda?"

"No."

"Why not?"

"Wasn't my place to butt in."

"No? Weren't you two 'family'?"

Minoru touched the corner of his mouth and laughed. "Hardly." He spat the word out. "Look, all we did was play a stupid game where we each took what we wanted from the others."

"How so?"

"The idea was to cheer yourself up while accessing the site. To make yourself feel good, for as long as you were online, anyway. I'd always wanted a sister—a baby sister or a big sister, either way. That, and a dad I could talk to. That's what it was all about," he said, his voice dropping. "But it didn't work out that way in the end. It just got messy. So I was going to drop out." By the end of this speech his voice had sunk to a barely audible whisper.

"What about you?" Takegami asked Ritsuko. "Even after the get-together, you went on playing the game, without any change."

"Yeah, well . . . it was important to me."

"Important to you."

"Yes, because it was something I'd never had in real life. It's true, you know—about my parents and me not getting along."

"So you never gave a thought to Kazumi Tokoroda."

Ritsuko swept her hair back, and shook her head. "She wasn't there. I never saw her face, and I didn't know her from Adam. How was I supposed to know if there even *was* an actual person named 'Kazumi'?"

"Mr. Tokoroda told you about her."

"How was I supposed to know he was telling the truth? On the Internet, people say whatever they want. You can't tell. And just because we'd met and spoken face to face, that still didn't mean I knew anything about him, really, did it?"

"So you thought he might be telling stories?"

"Yeah . . . maybe it was just easier to assume he was, I don't know."

"Everyone in your pretend 'family' was able to maintain enough distance so you could all take the easy way out. Is that because it was an Internet-based relationship, do you think?"

"That sounds to me as if you're prejudiced against the Internet, Officer," cut in Yoshie. "You should know that relationships formed on the Internet can be every bit as valuable and warm as relationships in real life. It's not all lies and fabrication. Not seeing each other face to face, not being caught up in what you look like and who you are in society, means people can open up to each other on a deeper level. And out of that exchange can grow feelings of genuine caring and love."

Minoru said scathingly, "Who you trying to kid, lady?"

"You be quiet!" she fired back. "Maybe for you the Net is a place for practical jokes, but not for me!"

"Who's playing practical jokes? You stole my line. I'm telling you, you've got no call to talk like that to me. You just don't get it, do you, lady?"

Yoshie slapped her hand against the tabletop. "There it is again. 'Lady.' Lady, lady, lady! I've got a name, you know!"

"What's wrong with calling you lady? You mean you're not one? Oh, I know—you're a *frustrated* lady. You're sexually frustrated and unfulfilled, and that's behind everything you say and do."

"What do *you* know about frustration!" Yoshie cried, her voice a howl. "Women like me suffer agonies, thanks to people like you who sit around and make fun of us—did you ever think about that? For not having a husband or children, we're treated as non-persons. How could you possibly understand the feelings of a woman like me?"

A fleck of saliva from her mouth flew at Takegami.

"That's real life, and I tell you, I'm sick and tired of it! I'm worn out! But you have to keep going. You have to work to eat. I know people at work look at me funny. But what else can I do, but go on working? Where can I go?"

Ritsuko was staring at Yoshie wide-eyed, dumbfounded.

"I needed a place to escape. That's why I enjoyed our family game so much. It was fun to be 'Mom,' even if it was just on the Net. I felt as if my whole life had changed—and that was enough to make me happy."

That was why she couldn't fathom the feelings of Kazumi Tokoroda. Couldn't begin to imagine them. In fact, not content with knowing Mr. Tokoroda only through the Internet, she'd begun to seek him out in real life as well . . .

"I don't know enough about Internet society to have any prejudice about it, one way or the other," said Takegami quietly. Yoshie's cheeks were flaming. "All I know is that given the proper catalyst, people will form relationships with each other. And just as truth and lies are mixed together in the real world, I'm pretty sure they must be in Internet society, too. That much I can tell."

Yoshie wiped the corners of her eyes with her fingers and then said, still more staunchly, "Our relationship was no lie."

Minoru and "Kazumi" were silent.

"Just suppose, for argument's sake," said Takegami, holding up his forefinger and then laying it on the end of his nose, "that before the murder took place, Kazumi Tokoroda had looked you all up and come to see you. What would you have done?"

Silence continued for several moments, until Ritsuko spoke up. "You mean she's a real person?"

"She most certainly is. A real person, made of real flesh and blood."

The three were silent again.

Takegami waited for the second hand to go around one full circuit, and then announced with a sigh, "Thank you for your cooperation. You're all free to go home for today."

Kazumi Tokoroda was weeping. The tears came coursing down her cheeks, one stream from the right and one, then two, from the left. She was standing still, so the teardrops hung from her jaw and then fell, landing on the toes of her shoes.

She still had her arms wound tightly around herself. Perhaps she did not even realize that she was weeping.

"Kazumi."

Chikako tapped her on the shoulder. The girl's mouth moved, quivering. What would she say? *Let it be the words we're after. Let this be the end*, Chikako prayed inwardly.

But Kazumi said only, "I want to go home."

Chikako felt drained. Her eyes dimmed with sorrow.

"Could you wait here a minute?" she said.

"I want to go home."

"There's one other person we'd like you to see."

Leaving Kazumi behind, she went to the interrogation room. Her feet were leaden, her back bent.

When the door opened to reveal Chikako, after one look at her face Takegami reached under the table and switched off the mike. She shook her head. "Call him in," she said briefly, nothing more.

Takegami gave the nod to Tokunaga, who started to reach out for the phone, and hesitated slightly. He did not look at Takegami and his hesitation lasted only a second, his hand swiftly grasping the receiver as if he had made up his mind. The look on his face, however, was stern. Takegami remembered what he had said before: *Isn't this a bit like twisting the arm of a baby?*

Right you are, my young friend, thought Takegami. *Because it's our job to twist arms when they need twisting, even if they do belong to babies.*

The guy was more upset than they had expected. He was attended by a cop, and Torii had an arm around his waist to support him. He was almost a head taller than Torii, who stood five feet eight inches, and his light brown hair, similar in hue to Kazumi's, stuck straight up all over his head like a baby's cowlick. The toe of one sports sandal caught on the floor of the interrogation room, nearly pitching him headlong. He staggered and caught himself.

Takegami stood up to greet him. "Ishiguro? Tatsuya Ishiguro?"

The youth nodded. His jaw hung slack. The rims of his eyes were red, and he was hitting himself in the side with his fist.

"Thanks for making up your mind to come in."

Tatsuya Ishiguro slumped down and swung his head loosely back and forth. What that might mean—whether it was negation or affirmation, confusion or resignation—was unclear. Until they heard his voice, no one could be sure.

"J-just let me see Kazumi, okay?" His voice trembled with profound pain and solicitude, such as no one else had shown so far that afternoon. "I've gotta see her. She's here, right? Let me see her. She and I have—"

"No way. It's a lie."

That's what Kazumi Tokoroda said aloud. How many times had she said it already now? Lies, lies, lies. To Kazumi it was all a big lie. Everyone and his brother had lied to her. Chikako said nothing in response. She only followed along behind the girl, keeping a close eye on her.

"Why . . . ?" murmured Kazumi, laying both hands on the glass of the two-way mirror. "Why? You said you wouldn't give in! You said you'd be fine! You said . . . what happened?"

Her hands moved, and struck the mirror. Once. Twice. Three times. Chikako flew over to Kazumi and dragged her away from the glass. Even so, Kazumi flailed wildly, trying to strike the mirror again.

On the other side of the mirror, Tatsuya Ishiguro heard the commotion and came over. His palms, more massive than Kazumi's, pressed flat against the surface.

"Kazumi. . ." His voice, picked up by the microphone, resounded through the room. "Kazumi, let's stop."

Kazumi continued to thrash about, tipping her chair over and sending her purse flying. The door opened and a uniformed officer rushed in. Chikako restrained him with a look and put her arms around Kazumi, holding her tight.

"Let's call it off." Tatsuya Ishiguro began to cry. His hands still on the mirror, he hung his head and wept. "We can't go on anymore. Okay, Kazumi? Let's call it off. It's over. Let it be over."

Still caught in Chikako's embrace, Kazumi collapsed and began sliding down. She hung her head and then, as if trying to make herself as small as possible, she buckled at the knees, scrunched her shoulders, and crouched down in a ball with her arms around her legs.

Chikako wrapped her arms all the way around the girl. She hugged her close, like a mother embracing her child at the end of the world.

Poster: Kazumi   4/4   10:39
Title: Let's meet again

Good morning! Is everybody out of bed? Or am I the first one up today?

Yesterday was fantastic! Did any of you notice those kids at the table next to ours? They thought we were for real! They had this look on their faces like, What a dopey, lovey-dovey family. But I thought they looked a tiny bit jealous too.

Anyway, now that we've all met, this is even more fun. We've totally got to do it again.

15

Kazumi Tokoroda's eyes were dry.

She wasn't looking at anything or anyone. Not at Chikako Ishizu in the chair next to hers, nor at Sergeant Takegami across from her, nor at the walls or windows or chairs, nor at Detective Tokunaga's profile, blending perfectly into the background like the "stage equipment" he said he was.

She wasn't looking at the room at all. Her eyes stared into empty space. Into the tiny space contained within the clasped hands lying on her lap.

"How're you doing?" asked Takegami, for lack of anything better to say. What would a veteran interrogator do now? What would he say? Takegami knew how to place documents on file and how to organize files. He knew the proper procedure for making a report of an on-the-scene investigation. He knew by heart the application form for every type of court order, and could handle the necessary phraseology with practiced ease. But in an interrogation room, he was out of his element. Knowledge of what to say was a treasure buried at the side of a road he'd never taken. Too late now to go dig it up. He'd get nothing for his trouble but callused hands.

Barely half an hour ago, this same room had been full of invisible emotions of every kind. Some had floated lightly in the air; others had wrapped around Takegami's neck or lain hunched at his feet; still others had been plastered flat against the window bars, straining to get out.

Now they lay fallen on the floor, all buoyancy lost, all trace of the energy that had propelled them gone. Had he only the power, thought Takegami, he could surely look down and see what was left of them settled lightly in deep piles around his shoes. Their fragile bodies lay chill and stiff like dead butterflies, ninety percent wing. The empty space in the room was dead. The only living space now was confined between Kazumi's clasped hands.

He hoped she would not squeeze it to death.

"Where's Tatsuya?" she breathed, scarcely moving her lips. Her expression remained so still that Takegami thought for a second he'd imagined it, that in his desire for her to start talking he had begun hearing things.

"Where is Tatsuya?" she repeated, her eyelashes trembling slightly this time. Her gaze was still trained on her hands. One might have thought the question was for them.

After a quiet look at Takegami, Chikako Ishizu spoke up. "He's in another room."

Kazumi did not nod in comprehension or otherwise alter her vacant stare. Without moving, she said, "Let him go."

Takegami leaned forward slightly, shortening the distance between Kazumi and himself.

"Why?"

"He's got nothing to do with it."

"No?"

"I dragged him into it."

"He doesn't seem to think so."

Suddenly, Kazumi looked up. Her eyes went straight to the two-way mirror. "Is there someone in that other room now?"

"No, nobody's there."

"Yeah, right. More lies."

"It's the truth. See for yourself, if you want."

Kazumi showed a flicker of hesitation, then half-shrugged. Takegami was being on the level with her, so he had nothing to lose. "Want to go take a look?" he invited.

Chikako started to get up, but Kazumi shook her head.

"No, it's OK."

She stared again into the space cradled between her palms. *If I got up, went around behind her and looked in there with her, I wonder if I'd see something too,* thought Takegami.

"Are you sure you don't want your mother here?" asked Chikako. She'd proposed having Harue Tokoroda sit in on this session from the start, but Kazumi had dismissed the notion offhand.

"No!" came the impatient reply. "I don't need her." She was fine on her own, she insisted. Then she turned to Takegami. "Officer..."

"Yes?"

"When did you first suspect me?"

"Is that what you want to know?"

"Yes. Tell me."

"It may only hurt to find out."

"It's OK. I mean, what's the difference...?" Her voice trailed off huskily. "My feelings don't matter anyway. I just want to know where I screwed up."

Chikako lowered her eyes. Seated side by side, the pair looked like mother and daughter, Takegami thought.

"We knew early on that you'd been poking around in your father's computer," he said. "Even before we ever checked the contents of the hard drive."

Kazumi's nose twitched. The skin of an adult would have formed a crease, but this girl's young skin was innocent of any such marks.

"We had your fingerprints on file. Remember? We took your mother's, too. When we checked Mr. Tokoroda's possessions for fingerprints, we had to eliminate the family first of all."

"Yeah, I remember."

"You got black ink all over your fingers, right?"

"It wouldn't come off and wouldn't come off."

"I know. In case we touch something accidentally at the scene of a crime, we have to be fingerprinted too. Those ink stains are tough to wipe off."

"So you're saying my prints were all over Dad's computer?"

"That's right. And Mr. Tokoroda wasn't at all security-minded. Anybody who had a mind to could have accessed all his files. So we put two and two together."

Although frankly it had never occurred to any of them that Ryosuke Tokoroda would leave his personal files unprotected, despite knowing that his daughter was snooping around.

"I never worried about fingerprints." Her voice was flat. "I just figured the computer belongs to the family, so if my prints are on it, big deal."

"That's right. That's what we thought, too. Probably lots of families share a computer. So at first no one suspected you. Until quite recently, we weren't even going to bring you in for questioning."

This apparently was a surprise. Kazumi raised her face and looked at Takegami.

It was a vastly different face from the one she'd shown him earlier in the day when, still knowing nothing, still having been told nothing, she'd first come in and said hello. Much of what he'd seen then was gone . . . clearly, unmistakably gone. The tension, the excitement, the wariness.

Most of all, the anger.

"In the early days, just for a little bit, we suspected your mother."

Kazumi nodded. "She told me. She said, 'The police think it's me. Not that I blame them.' She was all resigned about it."

"Yeah, well, because of the involvement of Naoko Imai, naturally we suspected her to begin with."

"But you never even questioned her."

"No. For one thing, there was the eyewitness testimony of Tomiko Fukada, the one who filed the initial report of your father's death. Mrs. Fukada—you know who she is? A lady in your neighborhood."

"No, I don't . . . think so."

"That doesn't surprise me. At your age, you probably wouldn't have any cause to know her. But your parents did. Tomiko Fukada knew your mother quite well. Even at night, even from a distance, if it'd been Harue Tokoroda who pulled back the plastic sheeting and stepped out, she'd have known."

"There you go," said Kazumi, as if to herself. "It's that simple."

"Besides, no matter how often we asked, or what corner we poked around in, there was never any sign your mother had an inkling of the affair between Naoko Imai and your father. And when we told her he'd been seeing a college student, she showed no particular surprise. So yes, at first we had our suspicions, but—"

Takegami chose his words carefully.

"—we got the distinct impression that your parents had declared a truce long ago over your father's extramarital affairs. Gradually, the picture filled in. That sort of marriage is pretty unusual, but not unheard of. Under the circumstances, it just didn't seem likely that Harue Tokoroda would suddenly up and kill first Naoko Imai, then your father."

"That's why she wasn't a suspect?"

"That's why."

"Then an apathetic life like hers has its uses after all."

She was not being ironic. She was merely making an observation.

"I'd say your mother and father each respected the other, in their own way," said Takegami.

Kazumi remained stony-faced.

"And it wasn't long before we came up with a new suspect," he went on, his voice mild as ever. "As you know, there was a young woman mixed up in a love triangle with Naoko Imai. A minor. She soon turned into our primary suspect. Everyone's attention zeroed in on her."

"'Miss A,' you mean," said Kazumi. "Lucky for the police her name never came out, wasn't it? You could have been sued."

"If that had happened, it would be the media that got in trouble, not the police."

"Now they'll be calling *me* that, won't they?" Kazumi gave a slight titter. "Little Miss A."

No one shared her amusement. Kazumi laughed alone, and then fell silent.

"You want anything to drink?" Takegami asked.

"No, thanks. Can I ask you something else?"

"Shoot."

"When did you track down . . . you know, them?"

"Them?"

"The Internet family."

"It wasn't me who located them, but with their email addresses to go on, apparently it wasn't too tough. A matter of going through procedures. We must have nailed them by, oh, a week after the murders, I'd say."

"Really?" She returned her gaze to the space between her palms. "A job like that is simple for the police, huh? Boom, boom, and it's done."

There were plenty of things Takegami could have said to that, but he held back, waiting to see where she was going.

"That woman, Yoshie Mita."

"Yes?"

"The other two suspected her. Didn't the police think she was at all suspicious?"

"Sure we did."

"Did you question her?"

"Yes, and it turned out she had an airtight alibi for the night of your father's murder."

Kazumi's eyes widened. "She did?"

"She'd gone to Osaka for a three-day training session. Left Tokyo the night before it happened."

"I never thought about alibis."

"You're not alone. Most people don't. Anyway, she was lucky. Not every major suspect in a murder case can come up with an alibi like that."

"Gosh," said Kazumi, like a little girl. "So everyone else was eliminated, leaving Miss A the only official suspect?"

"Yes."

"Then where would I come in? Although I guess technically I was never out, either. . ."

"Very astute. You have a good head."

"My grades are good," she acknowledged, without any change in expression. "I'm not stupid. That's why I can't abide stupid people."

"Oh?"

"I hate people who don't use their heads. Like my mom."

Takegami shifted his gaze to Chikako. She too was looking down at the space sheltered between Kazumi's palms. *What do you see there, Ma?*

"Actually," said Takegami, rearranging himself in his chair, "I'm standing in for someone else today."

"You are?"

"Uh-huh. Originally, someone else was supposed to be here in my place. A long-term veteran of the force."

The one who wrote the script for this little drama.

"He was the first member of the investigation squad to look at things from your point of view."

"*My* point of view?"

"That's right."

"So what did he think?"

The question was asked with an intensity she had not shown before. Takegami imagined he saw a small winged creature flutter up out of the tiny space cradled in her palms, and alight on her shoulder.

"His name's Nakamoto, but we all call him Naka. One time he said to me, 'You know, why doesn't anybody stop to think what it's been like for Kazumi? Why doesn't anyone look at it from her side?'"

—We're looking for someone with a motive to kill Ryosuke Tokoroda, right? In other words, someone who had feelings for him in spades. Feelings strong enough to commit murder for. Isn't that right?

She's right under our noses, he'd said. The girl snooping around in her father's computer.

"'See, if I was her, I'd be outraged. Furious. How could you possibly not be outraged about treatment like that?' That's what Naka said."

—Apparently Ryosuke Tokoroda was in a state of cold war with his daughter. That in itself doesn't tell you much. Anybody with a teenager in the house goes through a time like that. But this got out of hand. There's no way to laugh off what he did, even if it was done mostly online. Ryosuke Tokoroda procured a young woman with the same name as his daughter, hung out with her, and let Kazumi know exactly what he was up to. That's a hell of a way for a parent to act. Anybody on the receiving end of that treatment would be humiliated. Devastated. Why doesn't headquarters see that?

"'If I was Kazumi Tokoroda, I'd be so angry I couldn't see straight'— those were his exact words."

Kazumi's eyes opened wide, still staring straight down between her palms. But her hands were trembling, as if at any moment they might turn into fists.

Don't crush it, Takegami pleaded silently. *Open your fingers, let it fly away.*

But Kazumi could never have confronted her father with her anger. If she did, he'd only think she was caving in. That's what he was after, all along. "See there? You're Daddy's girl after all, aren't you? You don't like me spending time with any other little girl, do you? You're mine and you'll do as I say, won't you? There, now, that's a good girl. As long as you see how it is." That's the whole reason he did it, just so he could say those words to Kazumi someday.

Ryosuke Tokoroda lived his whole life like that. The connections he formed with people were all about *him*. He always had to be center stage. He never wanted people to be more than satellites, circling around him.

Only Kazumi—his own child—had had the nerve to reject that pattern and push him away. As any other perfectly normal adolescent child would do. But Ryosuke Tokoroda wasn't having any of that. He decided to tame his daughter, the same way he'd tamed his wife. And he picked the meanest way possible to put her in her place.

"If I was Kazumi Tokoroda," Naka had summed up, "I'd be hurt, and angry, and determined to find out just who was helping my father pull off such a nasty trick. What sort of person, nameless and faceless, could be sharing in this sick fantasy of his that was like some dirty toy in the shadow world of cyberspace? If I was her, I wouldn't rest till I knew. I'd make it my business to find out. And when I did, I'd give whoever it was a dose of reality, right where it hurt. You bet I would."

Takegami recounted all this to Kazumi, just as Nakamoto had said it to him, concluding with a direct quote: "'So I figure those two murders were just unlucky accidents that happened as part of that process.' That's what he said. But headquarters wasn't buying it. They were too hard-headed to even understand a motive like that. It was a whole lot easier for them to go for the classic motive of jilted lover; the one Miss A was wearing around her neck."

Takegami pursed his lips. The room was suddenly silent. And yet even amid the silence, he could hear a faint rustling of wings from the emotion that had flown up out of Kazumi's clasped hands before.

Surely Kazumi heard it, too. She must be able to hear it more plainly than he could. With her head tilted slightly to one side, eyes narrowed to slits, she listened to the beating wings of the emotion that had flown out of her inmost self, and then slowly she opened her mouth.

"It was all a mistake."

A case of mistaken identity, she said.

"I was . . . keeping my dad under surveillance."

"I know."

"And when the four of them arranged that get-together, I walked out of an exam and went to Shinjuku. Because that's where they'd all be. I'd be able to check them all out at once. Get a look at their faces. I even thought of barging in on their little party."

Takegami gave a deep nod.

"But as it turned out, I was too late. I missed them. It killed me to think I'd lost my big chance. I got really flustered."

"You couldn't have waited for the next opportunity to turn up?"

"That's what I should've done. But gee whiz . . . it's really hard, isn't it?" Sounding childishly plaintive again, Kazumi looked Takegami squarely in the face.

"What is?"

"Tailing someone."

"Ah, yes."

"I couldn't do it during the week, but on weekends, whenever my dad went out, I did my best to follow him. And every time, I'd lose sight of him, or else turn right around and come home because he'd almost seen me."

"That's understandable."

"The one time it worked, he went to Jewel."

And so she had witnessed Ryosuke Tokoroda in intimate conversation with Naoko Imai.

"I was positive she was 'Kazumi.' Totally convinced."

Ryosuke Tokoroda had, after all, sent "Kazumi" a message saying he wanted to see her again.

"That day I found out her name, and learned she was working there, and then—"

Came back later. With Tatsuya Ishiguro in tow.

"I'd told him everything. He was worried about me, and tagged along."

"Wearing a millennium blue parka."

"Yeah." She wiped her mouth with her hand. "He got that at a recycle shop, but the color was so loud he didn't like it much, and put it away. That night he had it on, though." Her tone weakened. "We weren't exactly going out for a picnic; maybe that's why he decided to wear something he never usually did."

"What did you mean to do when you found her?"

"Take her off somewhere so we could talk."

"She might not have wanted to go."

"She didn't. But I was prepared to use force if I had to. That's why I . . . took along the plastic rope." Kazumi closed her eyes. "My mom absolutely never throws any away. She winds scraps into a ball. Whenever she gets a new one, she ties it on and saves it. That's what I took along. I thought I might have to tie Naoko up."

"So what was it like, meeting her?"

"She was a real bitch."

"Ah."

"As soon as I talked to her, I figured out she wasn't the other Kazumi. But she *was* seeing my dad. And she recognized me."

"She did?"

"Yeah. She said she'd seen a photo my dad showed her."

—So this is little Kazumi! Well, well, well!

"She laughed at me." Head lowered, Kazumi opened her eyes. "She looked at me, and pointed, and laughed."

What was so all-fired funny? What was she laughing at? What in God's name had the two of them, that bitch and my father, been laughing at together?

"So I hit her. I must've really walloped her. She fell down and tried to crawl away. The look on her face changed. But I . . . I . . ."

Kazumi clenched her fists. But there was nothing left in them to crush anymore. One by one they'd come slipping through the cracks between her fingers, wafting their way upwards. Fragments of her heart turned to an invisible torrent, spewing into the void.

"I'm the one who killed her," Kazumi said in a small voice. "Tatsuya didn't do anything."

Chikako nodded, ever so slightly.

"Dad knew."

Her fists were still clenched, but the torrent had subsided. Her eyes stared into space. She was seeing her own turbulent emotions.

"He knew it was me who'd killed Naoko Imai. A little bird told him, I think. I could tell from the way he acted around me. So that night, it was my idea for us to meet there at the housing construction site. I told him I didn't want to talk at home, that it would just worry Mom."

"And you had Tatsuya Ishiguro go with you again?"

Kazumi twisted her mouth and nodded in assent. "Sorry," she said softly. This apology was presumably meant for the absent boyfriend.

"Who did the knife belong to?"

"I bought it."

"You did?"

"Yes."

"What for?"

"To be able to . . . resist my dad."

"You thought he was going to hit you?"

"Not hit me, but I thought he might turn me in to the police."

"Once you'd talked to your father and told him how you felt, weren't you going to turn yourself in?"

"Actually . . . I didn't think he'd be so upfront with me."

"Upfront about what?"

"About who they really were. 'Kazumi' and the other two."

"You mean to say that even after what happened with Naoko Imai, you still had to know?"

Kazumi said nothing. In a flash, Takegami felt as though he'd caught a glimpse into the core of her soul, a realm unknown to herself—filled with stubbornness, malevolence, burning hatred, and deep intransigence.

"That was the whole idea," Kazumi Tokoroda said with unshakable determination. "I wanted to meet each of them, one on one, and tell them everything. Let them know that because they toyed with me, I killed someone. I wanted my dad to see that, too. I was so determined to make him listen, I'd have threatened him with anything."

In that place and time, why couldn't she have taken a half-step back? Why couldn't she have made even the slightest effort to see the situation from a different angle?

"But Dad said he'd cover up what I did." From Kazumi's right eye, a single tear spilled out. "'You're my flesh and blood,' he said; 'if I don't look out for you, who will?' He said he'd never turn me in to the police, and he told me not to worry about Naoko Imai anymore, that it was all a bad dream and I could just forget about it now. . ."

I'll protect you. I'm your father.

"What a bunch of crap."

Her tears were falling freely now.

"He didn't get it. Nothing had changed. He was just sweet-talking me, the same way he'd done with the other Kazumi, manipulating me the same way he did her . . . them. I'd killed someone, I was hurt, and down, so he figured he could manipulate me, too—that's all it was!"

That's why I killed him.

"Hey."

"Yes?"

"Was it also Sergeant Nakamoto who figured that if you showed me 'Kazumi' and the rest of them, I'd get in touch with Tatsuya?"

"That's right."

"You didn't think I did it alone, then?"

"No, we didn't. We knew you were dependent on him, and that after your father's murder you'd sworn to him you'd get revenge, even threatening to kill whoever was responsible."

Harue Tokoroda had interpreted that outburst as an expression of Kazumi's anger against the unknown assailant.

"Most people who lose a close relative in a violent crime don't express anger that quickly. Like your mother, for example."

"Oh. . ."

"I'm not saying a young woman like yourself is incapable of murdering someone without assistance. It just didn't seem a likely scenario in this case."

Her cheeks wet with tears, Kazumi shook her head. "Still, there was no way for you to be sure I'd call him from here."

"No. But you did."

"Yeah . . . you know why? Because when you read out their names and all, I thought if I took notes, it'd look funny."

"So you sent him the information by email, over your cell phone."

"Yeah."

"Right on cue. Just like Nakamoto said you would, I mean."

—*Kids that age have no use for paper and pencil. Just let her have a cell phone and she'll use it, believe you me.*

"So that's why the police had him staked out?"

"That's right."

"Why—in case he got cold feet?"

"Not really. You see," said Takegami, "you still hadn't given up. Whatever it took, you were going to find out who those people really were. Weren't you?"

"Yes."

"And after we learned about their existence—when it became clear that Ryosuke Tokoroda had created an alternate family on the Internet—that's when you came up with your eyewitness story, right?"

"Well, I—"

"You figured we'd track them down for you."

"And you did."

"We sure did."

"That part about the stalker, though I just made that up."

"Wanted to throw us off, huh?"

"Yes. I still didn't know about Miss A or anything. I had to do *something* to throw you off my trail."

"Okay. . ."

"But then you all actually *believed* me, and put a protective guard on me, so. . ." She looked a trifle embarrassed. "I thought if I could pull the wool over your eyes again, you'd go out and find 'Kazumi' and the others."

"But you were dead wrong about something else."

"What's that?"

"Your boyfriend wasn't willing to play along anymore."

Kazumi bit her lip so hard it turned white.

"Just knowing you'd come here today was enough to make him antsy. Then you went and emailed him the real names and addresses of 'Kazumi' and the other two—just when he was ready to call it quits. He wanted it to be over, you see."

"If it wasn't for that parka, though, he'd have been fine!" An uncanny gleam lit her eyes. "He'd have stood his ground if *that* hadn't come to light!"

"Maybe so."

It was serendipitous that the parka had been found today of all days. But even without that bit of luck, just following Nakamoto's plan, they'd been planning to introduce false testimony in the course of the interview to the effect that Tatsuya Ishiguro had been spotted in a bright blue parka.

—Dammit all, I hate using a flat-out lie.

Nakamoto had fretted over the subterfuge, which laid bare the essential flimsiness of their elaborate scheme. Not that it was at all unusual for police to feed lies to suspects in custody. But Nakamoto, during his long time away from police questioning, had lost his taste for such sordid practices.

Today's discovery of the parka had thus seemed to vindicate Nakamoto's persistence and tenacity.

"Huh. So you're saying I fell straight for the game you played. Walked right into your trap."

He couldn't fault her choice of words. That was precisely what had happened.

"Don't be too sure of yourselves," she warned.

"How's that?"

"I'm still burned up. I might not drop it that easily. I haven't forgiven them."

"The shadow family, you mean?"

"Yes. I'm still a minor, with my whole life ahead of me. You can't do anything to me. After I'm released I might just go around and pay them all a visit, and you can't stop me. And whatever happens, the police department will be held accountable."

Childish strutting. That's what it was, he knew, and yet Takegami felt his heart sink all the way down to his shoes.

How ironic. Kazumi Tokoroda was her father's daughter, after all. She had supreme faith in herself, relied on herself implicitly—and would stop at nothing to get her own way.

Maybe it's the age we live in, he thought. *Me, me, me. Everybody and his brother hell-bent on finding their goddamn "true self." People who think they know all the answers choosing to fulfill their self-assigned mission in life by any means available, with total disregard for the feelings of others. What can you do?*

"They weren't real, either," Takegami told her. "It was all staged."

Pure astonishment covered her face. *"What?"*

"All three of them are members of the police force. 'Kazumi' and Minoru were played by a pair of fresh recruits. We were a little afraid they might not come off as teenagers. Everybody was pretty nervous about it, if you want to know."

The contents of their talk in the interrogation room had corresponded strictly to what had previously been gleaned from the actual Internet family—"Kazumi," "Minoru," and "Mom." It had been rearranged and repackaged, yes, but it was genuine for all that. The rest was sheer fabrication, he told her.

"Including everybody's names, addresses, and occupations, of course. So basically, nothing's changed. You'll never find the real Internet 'Kazumi' or Minoru."

You're better off that way. Better off forgetting the whole thing. If anybody had said anything like that to Kazumi before, perhaps she might have taken a different path.

"Wait a minute." Kazumi was half out of her chair. "What about that other email? The one my dad sent to Yoshie Mita. I *saw* it. That wasn't fake. That wasn't a lie. You didn't make that up. Are you telling me she's not 'Mom'?"

Chikako took over for Takegami. "No, the woman named Yoshie Mita is not 'Mom.'"

"Then you tell me who she is!"

"She's Miss A."

Kazumi pressed her hands to her cheeks.

"She had some strong reservations about your father. But she went ahead and wrote to him to resolve the problems she was having with Naoko Imai. That mail was his reply."

There'd been a good chance that Kazumi had seen that communication. So today they'd had to skillfully weave the name "Yoshie Mita" into the act. When working up the script, Nakamoto had been at pains to do that.

"You know how your father and she met, don't you?" Chikako went on.

After the meeting in the coffee shop, he had apologized for Naoko's behavior and offered to be of assistance, handing Yoshie his business card.

"She must have made up her mind to accept his offer. To anybody looking to build a case against her, that email is circumstantial evidence that she made an overture to your father . . . and that she could have killed him. But Kazumi, dear, look at it this way."

Kazumi was sitting stupefied, her arms hanging slackly, barely listening.

"Your father had his faults, there's no doubt about it. But a lot of people depended on him. However Yoshie Mita came to know him, her eventual turning to him for help is a sign that she responded to something positive in him. A kind of compassion, maybe."

"*Compassion?*" Kazumi's eyebrows shot up, as if she could not let the word go by unchallenged.

"That's right. It often happens that a person's faults, looked at another way, are also strengths. Your father was a compassionate man."

"Is that why he offered to cover up for me?" Kazumi's voice held not a spark of warmth. "That kind of compassion I don't need."

"All right, then, what is it you *do* need?"

There it was. What did Kazumi Tokoroda need?

"*What's right,*" she answered. "Justice. Anybody who hurts somebody for the fun of it has to pay for what they did. That's all. It's common sense. That's all I ever wanted."

No one—no one at all—who betrays and hurts me can ever be forgiven.

You're talking about revenge, not justice, Takegami started to say, but thought better of it.

If they went after Tatsuya Ishiguro, they might get what they wanted easily, without going through this whole charade. That's what he'd thought at first. A guy was more likely to crack, he'd argued, but Nakamoto had voted him down.

—My gut tells me that in this case, that wouldn't work.

—Why not?

—Kazumi Tokoroda is a strong-willed young lady. She could never forgive someone who turned her in, no matter who it was. No, if we're going to set a trap, it's got to catch her and her boyfriend both. Anything else is too risky.

Takegami envisioned Kazumi's stricken face and her fists, pounding on the two-way mirror as she screamed, "Why? Why? Why?" Here again, Nakamoto had been right. *Naka old buddy,* he thought, *maybe this is where you belong, back on interrogation.*

Chikako Ishizu sat for a while beside Kazumi, chin in hand, nodding her head as if she were remembering something. Presently she said, "Justice. Now there's a beautiful word." Her voice remained gentle. "But you see, Kazumi, I once knew a woman who believed in justice even more strongly than you do . . . and who only ended up killing a great many people as a result."

This was a reference to a central character in the case that had led to Chikako's demotion. Takegami had never heard Chikako talk about it before. He'd never even heard of her talking to anyone else about it, either.

"She was a young woman, like you," Chikako went on. "Her life did not come to a happy end, I assure you. Even now, that's something I find . . . deeply regrettable."

"Well, I don't have regrets," said Kazumi.

Which was real? That whispered "Sorry," before, or this?

Even after Kazumi had left the room, Takegami continued to sit unmoving, his ears tuned for the lingering reverberations of her voice in the walls, deep in thought.

"Kazumi" had said that being part of a family on the Net had been fun. That she'd gotten something from it she could have gotten nowhere else. That it had really meant something to her. "Mom," too, had indicated that the game was a source of consolation in her solitary life. Even Minoru, for all his defensive posturing, had been unable to tear himself away from that shadow family, probably an indication that through it, his lonely dream—"I always wished I'd had a dad I could talk to"—had, however incompletely, come true.

What if Kazumi Tokoroda had ventured onto the Internet? The thought was futile, but Takegami let his mind explore it. What if, without revealing her face or the sound of her voice, able to hide in the safe anonymity of a screen name, she'd had the chance to tell someone how she felt? Without revealing her eyes dark with anger or her mouth twisted in a grimace of distress, if she could have communicated those feelings in words alone, holding nothing back—what then?

Tatsuya Ishiguro, swept along by Kazumi for the simple reason that he was a flesh-and-blood creature capable of real-world action, had not been able to do anything for her. Perhaps someone out in the vastness of cyberspace might have. Beyond her reach, and remote enough to escape being caught up in her machinations, another person might have spoken to her, might have calmed her, might have understood her anger.

Perhaps she might even have found someone who would have shown her the sympathetic understanding of Nakamoto.

The interphone rang. After a brief exchange, Tokunaga reported, "The chief wants to see you."

"Okay." *Oh boy, here we go*, thought Takegami, stretching his back.

"Is Detective Ishizu all right?"

"What do you mean?"

"Nothing. What she said before. . ." Tokunaga drew up his shoulders. "That old case still seems to be haunting her."

"Yeah, well, who knows?"

Tokunaga muttered something to himself, and then said, "Oh, I forgot to tell you. Nakamoto's condition is unchanged."

"They said that just now?"

"Yes. Akizu checked with the hospital."

"He'd better come round pretty soon. I want my regular job back."

The one-act play they'd all staged together was finally over. How long was the mastermind going to stay asleep? *Get well soon and hurry back,* Takegami thought. *And hear the tale of my struggles as your understudy.*

But no, first on the agenda would be for him to meet Kazumi Tokoroda. Nakamoto should meet her in person and tell her in his own voice the words that only he could say.

"What was it like, becoming an actor overnight?"

"I'm not cut out for this."

"Don't be too sure. You were terrific."

"The only reason I could do the questioning was because I knew it was a sham. I could never handle the job for real." *I'm a desk pro.* "Those other three deserve a real hand, though. They did great."

"They'll never experience anything like that again in their whole careers, that's for sure," said Tokunaga.

Takegami grinned. "If you ask me, the one who played Yoshie Mita gets the prize."

"You think so?"

"Hands down." He mimicked her delivery. "'Do you have any idea of the agonies we women suffer?' You'd better see to it she sings a different song after this."

Tokunaga blenched. "All right, who let the cat out of the bag?"

"My sources are top secret."

"Damn, you have big ears."

Takegami heaved himself up out of his chair. It struck him how tired he was.

Tokunaga sprang up with far greater agility, glanced at the window and said curiously, "Son of a gun!"

Takegami looked back. Tokunaga had laid his fingers on the bars. "It's a butterfly. A cabbage butterfly."

Wherever it had come from, the butterfly was perched on a bar, its white wings folded.

"A sure sign of spring." Tokunaga tapped on the bar, and the white butterfly rose lightly in the air. Like a white petal, it was borne off on a current of air.

Dregs of all the emotions that had lain fallen on the floor of the interrogation room like numberless discarded wings . . . fragments of Kazumi's heart that had risen up out of her clasped hands . . . lies and truth. In Takegami's mind's eye, the image overlapped with the unsteady beating of these butterfly wings. Forlorn, solitary, pure white.

"'On the day when, at last, I journey into hell . . .'" Tokunaga said the words under his breath, with a slightly rhythmical cadence. "'. . . what shall I take to my mother and my father, and to the friends who are waiting for me there?'"

"What's that, a quote from something?"

"Yes. It's a poem I read once, long ago. I don't know what made me remember it."

What shall I take—

"So, what does the person take?"

"Huh? Let's see. . ." Tokunaga thought a moment. "'The pale, torn body of a butterfly.' That's it. Yeah, that must be what made me think of it."

To my mother and my father—

"'And as I give it to them, I know what I'll say,'" went on Tokunaga. "'My whole life, like a lonely child, this is what I chased.'"

He shut his mouth, stared up at the sky for a moment, and then closed the window.

"Let's go." Takegami tapped him on the shoulder. "We've got work to do."

（英文版）R. P. G.
Shadow Family

2004年10月22日　第 1 刷発行

著　者　宮部みゆき
訳　者　ジュリエット・ウィンターズ・カーペンター
発行者　畑野文夫
発行所　講談社インターナショナル株式会社
　　　　〒112-8652　東京都文京区音羽 1-17-14
　　　　電話　03-3944-6493（編集部）
　　　　　　　03-3944-6492（営業部・業務部）
　　　　ホームページ　www.kodansha-intl.com

印刷・製本所　大日本印刷株式会社